All thoughts flew out of her mind as Chelsea stared at Todd, unable to think of what to say. Those slightly crooked, strangely bright white teeth. That messy, I-live-on-the-water look to his light brown hair. The strong shoulders and arms. Oh yes, and that telltale smirk. It was Todd, all right. He hadn't changed a bit. But Chelsea had. She was his height now. And being able to see straight into his lake-blue eyes was suddenly extremely distracting.

Chelsea blushed at the awkward silence. She knew she had it bad.

Books by Hailey Abbott:

GETTING LOST WITH BOYS

THE SECRETS OF BOYS

THE PERFECT BOY

WAKING UP TO BOYS

SUMMER BOYS

NEXT SUMMER: A SUMMER BOYS NOVEL

AFTER SUMMER: A SUMMER BOYS NOVEL

LAST SUMMER: A SUMMER BOYS NOVEL

WAKING UP TO BOYS

Hailey ABBOTT

HARPER TEEN

An Imprint of HarperCollins*Publishers*

 Produced by Alloy Entertainment
151 West 26th Street, New York, NY 10001

Library of Congress Catalog Card Number: 2006933592
ISBN-13: 978-0-06-082435-8 − ISBN-10: 0-06-082435-2

Typography by Andrea C. Uva
❖
First Edition

Chapter One

Chelsea McCormick flew through the air, the cool water of Lake Tahoe stretching endlessly on either side of her. Grasping the boat's towrope with both hands, she squinted in the afternoon sunlight and shifted her hips, hopping from side to side over the boat's wake. As she gathered speed, she took a deep breath and jumped high into the air, grabbing the board between her legs. The lake was a blue blur below her.

For a long, luxurious moment, Chelsea was flying. The Northern California mountains looked like a smudged pastel drawing in the distance. There was nothing in the world she loved more than the heady, soaring feeling of being suspended over the water's surface. She never felt so much like a rebel as she did when she was defying the laws of gravity.

As her board touched down on the other side of the wake, Chelsea let a triumphant grin spread across her face. Everything felt right. Summer was beginning and she was in her favorite place in the world: out in the middle of the lake, wearing her favorite faded blue wetsuit and skimming her green Gator board along the frothy white surface of the wake.

Chelsea thought for the zillionth time how much happier she felt out on the water than on land. Here, she was a wild, graceful creature who could push her body to do even the most difficult feats. But back on land she felt like a too-tall, too-clunky, too-boyish behemoth who towered over all the other girls.

"You done back there?" her dad, Mark McCormick, called from the driver's seat of the boat.

"Never!" Chelsea shouted back at the top of her lungs.

Her dad gave her an apologetic look and pointed at the big waterproof watch on his wrist.

"All right." Chelsea sighed. She knew her dad had to prepare for summer staff orientation at Glitterlake Resort, the sprawling lakeside lodge and recreation complex he owned with her mom, and she'd already kept him out on the water for nearly two hours. Chelsea pulled herself back to the boat using the towrope and collapsed on the seat next to her dad. She ripped off her tinted goggles and squeezed the excess water out of her short brown ponytail.

"You looked good out there, Champ," her dad said, squeezing her shoulder.

"Yeah?" She smiled at the nickname he'd called her ever since she insisted on challenging the boys around the resort to tree-climbing contests when she was five. "How was my stance when I landed that jump? It felt a little wobbly."

"Looked pretty darn amazing," her dad said. "And if it was a little shaky, it was probably my fault for not lining up the wake better for you. But you can land anything, Champ."

He looked at her, grinning eagerly. She knew what he was thinking about: the Challenge. It was all that was on either of their minds ever since they'd learned that Glitterlake was hosting this year's Northwest Extreme Watersports Challenge.

Chelsea stretched her legs out over the boat's fiberglass floor, basking in the afternoon sun as they sped toward shore. Off in the distance, the resort's large windows glinted in the sunlight. From where she was sitting, the main lodge looked like an eagle resting on the crest of the hill—the lobby, dining hall, and reception rooms forming its body, and the east and west sections of guest rooms extending out on either side of it like wings. Gravel paths wound down from the main lodge to the clusters of cabins and waterfront tennis courts. Chelsea knew that behind the main lodge were the state-of-the-art indoor pool and spa, as well as her family's own comfortable home. Back beyond that, down another long gravel path nestled in the trees and tucked safely away at the foot of Pine Mountain, were the staff barracks, which, at that very moment, were probably filling with the last of the summer staffers, who'd be dumping their duffel bags on whatever remaining bunks they could find and noisily chattering about how their winters had gone.

The boat was rapidly approaching the docks adjoining the sandy beach that in just a few short days would be crowded with vacationing honeymooners and families. Now that Chelsea was sitting, she could feel the knots in her thighs from so much physical exertion, and she couldn't wait to get onto the dock and stretch. Maybe she'd even pop into Glitterlake's forty-jet Jacuzzi before the summer staff orientation meeting.

"Well, I know you're tougher on yourself than anyone, Chels," her father inserted into their comfortable silence. "But I just know you've got this summer's Challenge in the bag. I can feel it in my gut." He leaned back a little in his seat, slowing the engine as they got closer to the dock.

Chelsea's heartbeat doubled just thinking about it.

The Challenge was held at a different lake each summer, and the day she'd discovered that it was coming to Glitterlake was the most exciting of Chelsea's life. She'd been the first wakeboarder to send in her registration fee, and had spent all winter training and learning new tricks on her snowboard at Sierra Mountain. Not that snowboarding was nearly as rewarding to her as wakeboarding, but she had to stay in shape somehow, and Lake Tahoe was way too cold to brave in the winter.

"I'll be on the water every day until I'm ready." Chelsea heard the determination in her own voice.

Her dad smiled as he straightened out the boat. "That's what I like to hear," he said, turning off the engine and hopping easily onto the dock. He tied off the boat as Chelsea leapt out and began stretching her tight arms over her head.

"Okay, hon," her dad said, turning to head in the direction of the lodge. "I'll see you at the meeting later. Oh, and Champ?" He turned back to face her.

"Yeah?" Chelsea looked up and stopped stretching.

"I've got a couple of surprises I think you'll be happy about, so don't be late." She could see the huge smile her dad was trying to play down.

"Dad, wait! Do I get a hint?" Chelsea called, but he'd already started jaunting up the path.

She heard him laugh. "Then it wouldn't be a surprise!" he called back.

"I guess so," Chelsea said, her dad's smile now spreading to her own face. She really had the best dad ever. And there was no way she was going to let him down at the Challenge—even if it meant becoming a slave to her board. After all, she could think of worse things than that!

Chelsea was reaching down to her toes and taking deep breaths to relax her legs when she heard a shuffle, followed by, "Hey." Chelsea looked up and her heart dropped into her stomach.

There stood Todd Heron, the resort's reigning wakeboarding instructor, who also happened to be her crush of the past three years.

Chapter Two

All thoughts of surprises and her father flew out of her mind as Chelsea stared at Todd, unable to think of what to say. Those slightly crooked, strangely bright white teeth. That messy, I-live-on-the-water look to his light brown hair. The strong shoulders and arms. Oh yes, and that telltale smirk. It was Todd, all right. He hadn't changed a bit. But Chelsea had. She was his height now. And being able to see straight into his lake-blue eyes was suddenly extremely distracting.

Chelsea blushed at the awkward silence. She knew she had it bad.

"Earth to Chels," Todd was saying, waving his hand in front of her face. "Swallow too much lake water?"

Chelsea found herself laughing harder than she had when Justin Timberlake hosted *Saturday Night Live*.

"Long time no see," he said, coming toward her with his arms outstretched.

"Hey, man, I'm all wet," she said, laughing again nervously and shrinking back. She was sure that the last thing Todd wanted was a big water stain on the front of his faded hunter green Abercrombie tee.

"I can see that," Todd smirked. "How's the water?"

"Brilliant, as always," Chelsea replied, trying not to let her eyes linger on him too long. It was weird feeling this nervous around him. She'd always liked him, but he used to be so easy to be around.

"You looked pretty decent out there," Todd said, kicking at a splinter in the dock.

"Thanks. I didn't realize you'd seen me practicing." Warmth flooded her chest at the compliment. Todd was notoriously tough, saving his praise only for when it was really deserved. "I've been snowboarding my butt off all winter."

"Well, it shows," Todd assured her. "But the ending was a little wobbly on that last jump."

The critique was so typically Todd. "Think you could have done better?" she asked, narrowing her eyes at him.

"Is that a challenge?" He grinned. "Because you're not the only one who's been boarding her ass off all winter, you know. They could barely scrape me off the half-pipe back in Utah once all the snow melted."

"We'll see how you do on your first run," Chelsea retorted.

"Yeah?" Todd patted the large duffel bag hanging off his shoulder. "I've got a wetsuit right here if you want to put your money where your mouth is."

"I'm already wearing mine," Chelsea pointed out. She watched as Todd's eyes traveled down the length of her body, and she suddenly wished she hadn't said anything. There was no doubt that the suit molded to all the wrong parts of her long, lean frame, making her legs look scrawny and her boobs totally flat.

"Then I'll be right back," he said, slinging the duffel bag higher on his shoulder and heading toward the lakeside bathhouse. "And then let's get out on the water and you can show me what you've got."

As she waited for him to emerge, Chelsea couldn't tell if her heady, eager feeling of adrenaline was from the thought of another run behind the boat or from seeing Todd again. Of course, if it weren't for Todd, she might never have picked up wakeboarding in the first place. She'd been all about the skiing—on water and snow—until the hot new wakeboard instructor showed up at Glitterlake the summer she was fourteen and made her think that having both feet strapped into a single board might not be the worst idea after all—especially if he were there to make sure she stayed upright, his broad golden hands guiding her firmly as he barked instructions into her ear over the motor's roar. She honestly hadn't counted on falling so deeply in love with the sport itself . . . or on being so good at it. Before long she was trying jumps and grips that even Todd had trouble with. And, even though he had never come right out and said it, Chelsea was pretty sure that tough, competitive Todd wasn't wild about being upstaged by a girl.

"I can't wait to hit this lake," Todd said, swaggering out of the bathhouse in his wetsuit. Even though it came down to his ankles and zipped all the way up his neck, Chelsea's knees went weaker than after she'd landed her first 360. The suit's stretchy material clung to his body, hugging his chest and broad shoulders.

Todd hopped gracefully into the boat and extended his hand to help Chelsea off the dock. Normally there was no way she would let a guy think she needed his help to do *anything*, but the chance to touch Todd was too tempting. She rested her palm in his and felt the strength in his arm as he escorted her onto the gently bobbing craft.

As Todd leaned over to untie the rope from its slip, Chelsea slid into the driver's seat and started up the motor, feeling the boat sputter to life underneath her.

"So how was your winter?" Todd asked as she drove them out onto the water. "Do anything fun besides board your butt off?"

Chelsea gulped inwardly. The truth was, she hadn't—

in between spending every afternoon on the slopes and helping her parents out around the resort, she didn't have much of a life. But there was no way she was going to let Todd know that. "There's nothing more fun than boarding," she challenged instead.

Todd's sky blue eyes crinkled up at the corners when he laughed. "I concur," he said. "That's basically all I did, too. But, unlike you, I didn't have that pesky little thing called 'school' interrupting me."

"I'm so jealous," Chelsea sighed. Sitting in a classroom all day felt like torture when she could see the snowy peaks of Sierra Mountain sparkling in the distance. "School shouldn't be in the daytime. All that light goes to waste. I could make much better use of it out on the water."

"Well, someday you, too, could become a professional board bum," Todd joked, reaching out and pushing playfully at her shoulder. The contact made her insides turn to syrup, and a thought suddenly occurred to her. Was Todd . . . could he be . . . flirting with her? Was he teasing her because he could tell that she liked him? Or was it something more? Chelsea wondered if by some miracle he was starting to see her as someone in his league—someone more than just a wakeboarding student. Was it possible that Todd could think of her as a *girl* . . . like, the kind of girl he could flirt with?

Chelsea slowed down as they reached the middle of

the lake and let Todd climb out behind the boat. Even with his face half-covered in goggles, he was still the single hottest guy she had ever seen. "Well, feast your eyes on this," he said before sliding into the water, sending all her hopes and dreams about him seeing her as more than just the competition swirling down the drain.

Oh, I will, Chelsea thought, amused by how true his words really were.

She sped up the boat, watching the long white wake stretch out behind in the many rearview mirrors positioned to give the driver the optimal view of the rider behind. She was so used to the way he moved—they'd been practicing together for years, and she'd memorized the way his body worked.

She watched as Todd gathered momentum, swinging his body from side to side. She could tell from the way he was riding nearly fifteen feet outside of the wake that he was planning a big jump. Coming back into the wake, Todd stood up tall on his board and flipped suddenly into a double back roll, turning all the way upside down in the air. Chelsea winced as she realized he was underrotating, giving the towrope too much slack so that he didn't get enough of the natural speed of the boat. She sped up slightly, hoping to make the rope taut enough for him to land the trick successfully, but it was too late. Without the natural momentum of the boat's speed, Todd couldn't get all the way around. He skidded to a halt on his butt several feet outside the wake. Even over the motor's roar, Chelsea could hear him cursing.

She slowed down long enough for him to regain his footing and then took off again, watching his body language grow bolder and his moves more confident. She could tell he was going to try the double back roll again—and this time he was going to nail it. Sure enough, Todd's body flew through the air in a set of perfect cartwheels, his strong legs flexed high over his head. He landed expertly and flashed Chelsea a triumphant smile before using the towrope to pull himself back · toward the boat.

"Well, how was it?" he asked, climbing into the boat and shaking the water droplets out of his hair.

"You looked great!" She decided not to mention the butt-skid—even though she knew *he* would have mentioned it if their roles had been reversed.

"Man, it's good to be back here. I missed this place." Todd stretched his arms over his head so that his soaked wetsuit settled into the crevices between his hip and stomach muscles. He let his arms swing back to his sides and smiled down at her. "You ready to let me drive for a while?"

Chelsea stood up to give him the driver's seat. As she did, the boat rocked below them and Todd automatically reached out to steady her. She drew closer to him, her heart pounding as the boat's rocking gently subsided.

Todd's face was so close to hers that she could count the drops of lake water on his eyelashes. They stood that way in silence for a moment until he abruptly let go and slid into the driver's seat.

"Let's see what you can do," he said, casually resting an elbow on the wheel.

Chelsea smirked. "Oh, I'll bring it," she said, looking straight into his eyes.

Her heart still hammering, she slipped her feet into the bindings of her board and strapped it on nice and tight before sliding out into the water. Even though her body was tired from riding less than an hour before, she was determined to show him just how much she'd improved over the winter. After a few grabs, she felt confident enough to try a roll of her own. Taking a deep breath and heading way outside the wake, Chelsea launched herself into what had to be the most perfect double back roll in the history of wakeboarding. She landed well wide of the wake, her knees and feet rock-steady beneath her. She was about to do a little happy-dance when she caught a glimpse of Todd's frowning face in the rearview mirror. Chelsea's triumphant smile faltered and then disappeared. Was he upset that she'd landed the same trick he'd just messed up on, and on her first try? She suddenly felt the effort of the day's two practice sessions seeping through her tired muscles. She signaled him to slow down and dragged herself back into the boat. She sank into the passenger's seat and unclipped her bindings. Todd's forehead was still lined with a scowl, and his shoulders hunched over the wheel.

"Nice job out there," he said, looking straight ahead. She could feel the tension.

"Thanks," she replied, her heart sinking at the dreaded note of envy in his voice. She *knew* she'd looked great on the water. And she also knew that that just might be the problem.

Chapter Three

Chelsea hurried from her family's chalet-style house along the short gravel path to the main lodge, hoping she wouldn't be late to the orientation meeting. The sun was just starting to dip below the lake's surface, and the air had picked up a bit of high-elevation chill. She shivered slightly, wishing she'd remembered to throw on a track jacket over her Adidas T-shirt. Her mind raced with thoughts about Todd.

I need to suck it up and get over Todd already, she told herself, picking up her pace as she walked. It was time to move on and wake up to the other fish in the sea. As she shoved her hands deeper in her pockets, she vowed to herself that this would *finally* be the summer when she would move on, kick Todd's butt in the Challenge, and maybe even find herself a real boyfriend—the kind she could actually date outside of the fantasy world in her head.

"Chelsea?" a cheerful male voice shouted from several feet behind her on the path. Chelsea broke into a smile when she saw Leo Clarke, the lanky, scruffy-haired bartender from the Lakeside Lounge.

"How's my little resort rat?" he asked, wrapping her in a big hug so that her face scratched against the rough material of his flannel shirt.

"Who're *you* calling a resort rat?" Chelsea teased as they continued down the path, arm in arm. "I'm glad they managed to drag your butt off the mountain so you could join us this summer. How was Snowmass?"

"Sweet—poured a lot of beers, hit a lot of powder. Got a new pair of telemarking skis!"

Chelsea shook her head and chuckled. Like much of the resort's summer staff, Leo was a ski bum just looking to make a few extra bucks in the summer. His chill, personable demeanor made him the most popular bartender at the resort's watering hole.

"So hey," Leo said right before they reached the entrance to the lodge. "We're having a, uh . . . you know. Tonight. Out on the island. You in?"

A huge grin spread across Chelsea's face. She knew secret keggers on the lake's single island were a long-standing tradition amongst the summer staff, but this was the first one she had been explicitly invited to.

"Definitely," she said, trying to sound casual as Leo pushed open the heavy double-glass doors, letting Chelsea follow him into the lobby, with its rough-hewn hemlock beams, thick Indian carpeting, and tasteful nature photography. This early in the season, the place was devoid of tourists, but they both waved to Juanita at the front desk before heading up the sweeping staircase that led to the mezzanine.

The library was already full of summer staffers, excitedly greeting one another after a long winter apart. The crackle of voices and laughter competed with the loud hisses and pops of the fire roaring in the huge stone fireplace against the north wall. As Leo went bounding across the room to greet Tim from the Mountain Bike Shoppe, Chelsea looked around. Mel Boyer, who worked at the spa, caught her eye and waved, and Chelsea squeezed through the crowd to join her and Sienna Jameson, the other resident massage therapist.

"Hey, how was your winter?" Chelsea asked, giving both girls quick hugs.

Sienna laughed and shook her head. "I'm glad it's over!" she said. "The past semester nearly did me in."

"Seriously," Mel agreed. "We were both taking like eighteen credits *and* working. We totally need a vacation."

Just then Chelsea's parents bustled in and quickly dimmed and brightened the lights several times to indicate that the meeting was about to start. Chelsea hurried to the back of the room and slipped into a seat that was conveniently tucked between two high bookcases, hoping she looked inconspicuous. She always felt kind of embarrassed to be in the same room as her parents when they were doing their "We Own This Place and You All Work for Us" act. Most of the summer staffers actually raved about how cool Mark and Patty McCormick were to work for; she just didn't want to remind anyone of the connection—it made trying to blend in that much more difficult.

But now that she was finally old enough to get invited to the staff parties, maybe all of that would change. She hoped. She couldn't help wondering who would be at the party. Would Todd be there?

Stop, Chelsea reminded herself sternly. *You're not thinking about Todd anymore, remember?*

"Well, I don't know about the rest of you. . . ." Mark McCormick was already well into his standard staff announcements. Some girl—Natalie or Nina or something—had just said hi to everyone, but Chelsea's thoughts were still on the island party and her ride with Todd earlier, so she was surprised to suddenly hear a new voice. A very smooth, slightly accented voice—a *totally hot* voice. She peered past some heads to the front of the room.

The boy who had been introduced was standing

there. He had a smooth, olive-colored complexion, a strong jaw, and penetrating black eyes. Despite his angular features, he had a soft, playful smile.

"Hi, I'm Sebastian. It's great to be here," he started, softening his vowels and rolling his *r*s. "I am from Brazil, where I compete in tennis tournaments, including the South American Open. I've been playing since I was six, and teaching for three years, since I was sixteen. I am looking forward very much to getting to know all of you." As he said these last words, his gaze landed on Chelsea and lingered a moment.

Normally if a cute guy looked at Chelsea, she would have stared down at the floor, watching her Reefs shuffle back and forth. But this time she managed to hold Sebastian's gaze and even give him a tiny smile. Something clicked in her head just then. The way to get over an agonizing, pointless crush? Flirt with a cute stranger! Not that Chelsea really knew how to flirt properly, but that was beside the point. She could always learn. *Good-bye, Todd! Hello, hottie foreign tennis guy!*

Suddenly, Chelsea realized Sebastian wasn't the only person in the room looking her way. In fact, everyone was turning toward her, smiling and clapping. What was going on? What had she missed?

She realized her dad was directing his speech toward her. "Chelsea," he said in his warm, rich baritone, "I couldn't be happier to give you this promotion. After two years of lifeguarding, you've more than earned your place next to Todd as a wakeboarding instructor."

She heard Leo whoop, and Mel and Sienna grinned at her. A flush of pride and sheepishness hit her at the same time. Wakeboarding instructor! So *that* was her dad's surprise! *Awesome.*

"Thanks," Chelsea managed to stutter. "I'm honored." Understatement of the year. Her first island party, a promotion to wakeboarding instructor, and a hot new staff member who might or might not have been looking her way—things were certainly starting to look up. She smiled and took her seat as her father wound down his speech.

"Last, but—as you'll certainly agree—not least, I'd like you all to give a warm welcome to my other daughter, Sara," Mark boomed proudly.

Chelsea did a double take. *Sara?!* As in, her half sister, the total princess who lived in Palm Springs?

Sara, who had apparently been sitting near the front of the room all along, rose gracefully and turned to face the rest of the staff. "Hi, I'm Sara, and I hope you'll all join me for a hike around Glitterlake this summer." Sara smiled, absentmindedly smoothing the top of her platinum blond ponytail. "I've always loved plants, and I'll be starting as a botany major at UC Santa Cruz in the fall. I've lived and worked at the Desert Winds Resort and Spa in Palm Springs for most of my life, so I know my way around resorts . . . but I can't wait to get started giving nature tours here. I'm excited to work and hang out with all of you."

Even though Sara hadn't said anything that spectacular, Chelsea noticed that the guys in the room were hanging on her every word. She wondered if it was because of the chatty way Sara spoke, or because she happened to be a dead ringer for Scarlett Johansson.

Nature tours? Chelsea rolled her eyes. This must have been her dad's *other* surprise. This would be interesting.

Instinctively, she glanced toward where Todd was sitting to see how he was reacting to everything. But he was chatting to someone sitting next to him, oblivious to Chelsea. As always.

Chapter Four

Chelsea checked her watch—nearly midnight—and zipped up her fleece-lined warm-up jacket. Sliding her small Petzl headlamp into the pocket, she turned off her light and carefully closed the door to her room behind her, holding her breath as the door clicked softly shut. She tiptoed down the hall and paused outside the door of the room that had, up until that morning, been the guest room. Now it was Sara's room. Chelsea couldn't quite get used to the fact that her half sister was actually going to be living in the room next door to her for the summer. She hadn't even seen her since the eighth grade, and even then it had been obvious that they were—how to put this nicely?—two very different people.

Chelsea wondered if she should knock on Sara's door and invite her along—but then she realized that she hadn't seen Sara since the meeting earlier. It would probably just be awkward, and she didn't want anything to ruin the night ahead. Island parties had been a tradition for as long as Chelsea could remember, but as "the owner's kid," she had never been invited along. Maybe with her new promotion, they would start seeing her as one of them. Tonight was going to be the beginning of a whole new Chelsea in their eyes, and she couldn't wait. Then again, if she *didn't* ask Sara to come, too, would everyone think she was just being mean?

Chelsea stood outside Sara's bedroom door for several long seconds. She could tell from the dark crack under the door that the light wasn't on, and she couldn't hear any sounds coming from inside, so she figured Sara was asleep. She was probably tired from the trip, Chelsea decided. Besides, she was probably used to posh parties in clubs—why would she even want to go to an island party in the first place?

Chelsea continued down the hall and sneaked down the stairs to the front door, relieved that she didn't have to bring Sara along—just in case Sara might have told her parents. Chelsea had always wondered if her parents secretly knew about the island parties and had just decided to turn a blind eye as long as the staff didn't trash the island and nobody got hurt—but just in case they really didn't know, Chelsea didn't want to do anything to risk them finding out.

*   *   *

Down on the dock, Leo was directing a small crew as they loaded coolers full of beer onto the boats, guided by the beams of their mountaineering headlamps. Chelsea switched on her Petzl and grabbed an armful of firewood. She had just heaved it into the back of one of the boats when she saw Sara walking toward her, holding a bag of marshmallows and whispering with Sienna.

"What are you doing here?" Chelsea asked. She must have sounded harsher than she meant to, because both girls gave her funny looks.

"I was just hanging out at the barracks," Sara said. "I came with everyone else."

"Oh," Chelsea said. "Cool." Her cheeks flushed. Sara had been invited to the party, too? The same party Chelsea had been waiting her entire pathetic life so far to get invited to? Not only that, but Chelsea had been to the staff barracks only a handful of times. It had always felt to her like a secret clubhouse that she could never really belong to. Apparently Sara could.

"Everyone ready to go?" Leo asked. He grinned as Chelsea hopped easily into the driver's seat, and he then stopped to extend his hand to help Sara.

"Let's go," Chelsea whispered once the backseat was full. Mel, Sienna, Leo, and Sara all huddled together. They began to glide slowly out of the dock, and Chelsea waited until they were a good distance from shore before pushing the boat full-throttle. Cheers and giggles came from the back as a white wake sprayed up behind them, and soon the boat was skimming quickly over the water as a strong headwind whipped wisps of hair across her face.

Although she was concentrating on driving, Chelsea could hear snippets of the conversation behind her. Leo was telling a story about running into a bear on one of his backcountry skiing excursions, and everyone was alternately gasping and laughing at his comedic delivery. But then Leo did something he almost never did: He stopped in the middle of a sentence.

"Hey," he said to Sara. "You're shivering—are you cold?"

"A little," Sara admitted. "But it's my own fault. . . . I didn't realize how cold it gets in the mountains at night." Chelsea smirked. She had wondered why Sara hadn't changed out of her white sundress from earlier. Now, seeing the easy way that she flirted with Leo, Chelsea realized it was probably all part of Sara's scheme to have every guy on the planet fawn over her.

"That's why a mountain man like me always dresses in layers," Leo joked. He was already unsnapping his black-and-red-checked wool hunting jacket to reveal a thermal hoodie. "Rule number one about partying at high elevation: No matter how hot it is during the day, it still gets really cold when the sun goes down. Here, put this on." He handed the jacket to Sara, who gratefully slid her arms into its sleeves. She looked predictably cute.

Once he'd made sure that Sara was all right, Leo continued with his story, and Chelsea tuned out, wondering for the millionth time what the party would be like. Was that cute Sebastian guy going to be there . . . or—she couldn't suppress the thought—Todd? Would she be able to say the right thing without coming across as annoying?

She cut the motor and let the boat drift the last few feet to the island's rickety dock. There were already several other small motorboats docked there, some of which she knew didn't belong to Glitterlake. Word of the party must have gotten around to staff at the other resorts on the north side of the lake. The sound of guitar music and the smell of woodsmoke drifted down to the dock from the fire pit and Chelsea breathed it in as she helped unload coolers, thinking that the smell of a campfire was a sure sign that summer had really begun.

"This is spooky," Sara whispered as the group followed the wobbling beams of their headlamps up the well-trodden path to the fire pit.

"You can't seriously be scared," Chelsea said incredulously. But even as she said it, she realized that she was a little nervous, too. It was late and the woods on the island were dark. Plus, what if they got caught?

"I'm kinda spooked, too," another girl piped in. It was that girl from the meeting earlier, Nina or whatever. "But in a fun way. Like at a haunted house or something." Sara grabbed Nina's arm, and the girls charged ahead toward the sounds of music and voices.

The fire pit was set in the middle of an open grove of pine trees not far from the water's edge. For as long as anyone could remember, the pit had been surrounded by large flat stones and thick fallen logs, and an ancient picnic table rotted nearby. At the moment, a roaring fire illuminated the faces of the revelers, surrounding the group with an orange glow. Summer staffers from all over North Tahoe lounged, laughed, and chatted on the stones and logs, and the picnic table was piled high with snacks.

Chelsea's heart caught in her throat when she noticed Todd standing off to the side, the firelight illuminating his sharp, masculine face as he put his hands out to his sides, obviously demonstrating a new wakeboarding move to some guys from the Ridgetop Grille. Chelsea quickly took off her Petzl and ruffled her matted hair.

Instead of going over and listening to him brag about

how great he was on a wakeboard, though, Chelsea wandered over to the picnic table to grab a long stick and a marshmallow to roast. Tim from the Mountain Bike Shoppe looked up from where he was assembling s'mores and smiled, brushing his shaggy brown hair out of his eyes. "Hey, Little McCormick," he said, "long time no see. How's it going?"

"Great!" she answered, cringing slightly at the old nickname. She sat down to talk to him. But her butt had barely touched the bench before he lowered his voice and moved closer. "Hey," he asked, cocking his head in Sara's direction. "Who's that new girl you came up with?"

"Oh, that's my half sister," Chelsea explained, wanting to roll her eyes. She smoothed her hair out of her face. "She's here for the summer. She's doing plant walks or something."

"Really?" Tim looked at Sara wistfully. "Introduce me?"

"Sure, whatever," Chelsea said, feeling more than a little annoyed.

"Yo, Sara," Chelsea called over the din of people talking. Sara looked around and immediately headed toward them, smiling the social-butterfly smile that Chelsea could barely believe she would have to look at all summer.

"What's up?" Sara asked, giving Chelsea a perplexed look. A cold breeze rustled the trees around the fire, and Sara pulled Leo's jacket tighter around her shoulders.

"Oh—this is Tim. He wanted to meet you," Chelsea blurted. Tim kicked her under the table before smiling warmly at Sara and extending his hand.

"Chelsea never told me she had a sister," he told Sara. "I was curious to see what you're like."

"Half sister," Chelsea grumbled, running her finger against a heart with the initials *A* + *K* carved into the table. But nobody seemed to hear her. In the meantime, it looked like Tim might be blushing. It was hard to tell in the dark.

Tim's best friend, Ethan, joined them. At well over six feet, he towered above the group, his face shadowed by a fur-trimmed hunting cap. "Hey," he said, punching Tim lightly on the shoulder. "How's it going, man?"

"Can't complain, bro," Tim replied, punching him back and sliding a little closer to Sara.

"Hey, hi—I'm Ethan." Ethan held out his hand to Sara, who was still smiling politely. "So you're a McCormick, too, eh? Two Daddy's little girls we have to watch out for!"

Chelsea rolled her eyes. Tim had at least bothered to ask how Chelsea was doing, but Ethan—whom she'd known since the first grade—hadn't even said *hi* to her before falling all over himself to meet Sara. Ethan had always been a little overeager around girls, but this was ridiculous.

She tuned back into the conversation long enough to

hear Sara telling the guys that she was from Palm Springs.

"Is everyone down there like you?" Ethan asked. "Because if so, I need to take a road trip!"

Instead of blushing or telling him to shut up like Chelsea would have, Sara just laughed. "You guys should go check it out." She tilted her head and shook out her pale blond hair, which obviously acted as some kind of man-attracting signal, because three seconds later, Joel and Ted came bounding over, practically colliding with each other as they each dived to offer Sara a beer.

"Sorry, I don't accept drinks from strangers," Sara teased.

"But if I tell you my name, I'm not a stranger," Ted retorted playfully.

Chelsea felt sick to her stomach and wondered if anyone would even notice if she threw up. She grabbed her marshmallow stick and wandered away from the Sara Admiration Society and found an empty rock by the fire. Maybe she just wasn't the partying type. She knew these people, so why was she feeling so awkward? She leaned toward the fire pit, searching for a nice hot patch of coals to roast her marshmallows. The only way to do it without setting them on fire was to keep turning them steadily over a bed of glowing embers. She found a spot and began rotating the stick, letting the marshmallows grow brown and crisp.

But her technique was ruined as the smoke made her eyes teary. She was trying to wipe them without dropping the stick when she heard Todd's deep, throaty laugh.

Chelsea whirled around, inadvertently sending her nearly done marshmallow smack into a burning log, where it immediately incinerated. Todd was standing over by the coolers, talking to a girl with long dark hair. She wore a cream-colored blazer, dark jeans with black ankle boots, and had a small black leather backpack slung casually over one shoulder. Chelsea thought she looked like she had just stepped out of *Lucky* magazine.

"Vanessa, let me get this straight: You're terrified of *water*. And yet you let your so-called friends talk you into a vacation on Lake Tahoe?" Todd was asking, leading her closer to the secluded rock where Chelsea was sitting. Clearly, they hadn't noticed her sitting there.

The girl shrugged. "It was either here or Guadalajara," she said. "And I've been there before—I got food poisoning." She laughed easily, touching Todd's shoulder. So this Vanessa girl was *a tourist*. Todd had brought some tourist chick to the staff party. And they were all worried they'd get in trouble for having Chelsea there. Chelsea didn't know if she wanted to throw up or punch something.

Todd leaned closer to Vanessa. "And then these same friends let you go off with some guy you hardly know, to an island smack in the middle of said lake."

"I guess my safety is in your hands, then," the girl murmured, raising her eyebrows.

"I guess I'll just have to protect you, then. C'mere—I want to show you something," Todd said, taking her hand and leading her toward the woods. Chelsea winced—she could guess what Todd wanted to show that girl. It was a small wood cabin (that had probably been a hunter's hideout at some point) that the summer staffers around North Tahoe had dubbed the "Shag Shack." Even Chelsea had been privy to the stories. Apparently each year, someone made sure it was equipped with an air mattress and sleeping bag.

She watched as they disappeared into the darkness of the woods.

Chelsea's stomach felt like the empty black shell of her former marshmallow. There was no way Todd would ever be interested in her. She didn't have long perfect hair or cute clothes, she had no idea how to flirt, and she'd never even been near the Shag Shack. She was half-tempted to just get up and go home.

"Excuse me," said a voice so close to Chelsea's left ear that she jumped slightly. The new tennis instructor, Sebastian, was standing next to her, holding two ice-cold Sierra Nevadas, one of which he extended toward her. "I brought you a drink."

"Gee, thanks," Chelsea blurted sarcastically, still distracted by the image of Todd slinking off with Vanessa.

Sebastian's smile faded, and his big black eyes narrowed. "Sorry," he said softly. "I just wanted to talk to you. I'll leave you alone."

"Crap," Chelsea murmured to herself as he turned to leave. Sebastian was the only person at the party who had paid any attention to her at all. What was wrong with her?

"Hey!" she called after him. Sebastian turned, and she waved him back over with one hand. "I'm sorry," she said. "I'm kind of having a rough night. And I'm not used to being . . . Well, guys here aren't usually that direct."

Meaning guys aren't that direct with me, Chelsea thought.

"Do you mind if I sit down?" Sebastian asked.

"Not at all," Chelsea said, scooting over to make room for him on the rock. "And actually, I'll take that beer if you're still offering."

"Of course." Sebastian handed her the beer and sat down next to her. "Salut."

Chelsea clinked her bottle against his and took a gulp. "So, you're from Brazil, huh?"

"Yes." Sebastian nodded. "And you . . . where are you from?"

"Me?" Chelsea asked in surprise. Everyone knew where she was from. "I'm from here."

"Lake Tahoe?" Sebastian asked. "This town?"

Chelsea was about to open her mouth and tell Sebastian that she'd grown up right there at the resort when she realized something: Sebastian was probably the only guy at the party who wasn't making a big deal out of the fact that she was the bosses' daughter.

"Around here, yeah," she said vaguely.

Sebastian nodded, biting his lower lip in a really cute way. Chelsea noticed that he had very straight teeth. "And you're a wakeboarding instructor?"

"Well . . . this'll be my first summer teaching," Chelsea said. "But I've been boarding for years."

"You like it?"

"Love it," Chelsea said confidently, taking another sip of beer. "It's my favorite thing in the world. You feel that way about tennis?"

"Playing, yes," Sebastian said. "Not so much competing. But I *love* teaching. To see my students when they get it. There's a little spark when something I tell them just clicks. It's great."

"I'm a little nervous about teaching," Chelsea admitted. "I've never done it before. I'm not even that great with kids."

Sebastian shrugged. "It's not that hard," he said. "Just remember to make it fun. That's what summer vacation is about."

"I guess," Chelsea mused. For her, summers had always been about work: lifeguarding, practicing her wakeboarding, and helping her parents keep the resort running smoothly.

"Don't *you* like to have fun in the summer?" Sebastian asked, smiling. He leaned closer to her: so close to her that she could feel his breath tickling her ear.

Was it her imagination, or was Sebastian hitting on her? Chelsea couldn't be sure—it wasn't exactly like she got hit on every day.

"I guess so," she said quietly, inadvertently matching Sebastian's sultry, confidential tone.

"I certainly plan to," Sebastian said, locking eyes with her again.

"Yeah," Chelsea blurted out. "Er, I mean, yes. Me, too."

Chelsea was still trying to figure out what exactly Sebastian was thinking. She hoped she didn't seem as nervous as she felt, trying on this whole flirting thing.

A loud crash of branches behind them made her jump. Todd and Vanessa emerged from the woods, their fingers interlocked.

"I know, it's beautiful at night," Todd was saying. Chelsea's stomach curdled.

"Mmm, thanks for showing me," Vanessa replied, leaning over and kissing him gently on the cheek. "Want a beer?"

"Sure," Todd agreed.

As they passed Chelsea, Todd's eyes met hers for a few agonizing seconds and he raised an eyebrow at her, then looked away.

"Chelsea?"

Chelsea suddenly remembered that Sebastian was sitting right next to her. She focused her gaze on him and did her best impersonation of a sunny smile. "Yeah?" she asked.

"I was saying, it's a little smoky over here—want to go somewhere a little more quiet?" Sebastian asked, taking her hand in his warm palm.

Chelsea glanced over at Todd one last time. He was standing by the fire with his back to her and his arm draped over Vanessa's shoulders, laughing at something that one of the bike shop boys had said.

Chelsea took a deep breath. *Mission: Moving On begins. . . .*

"Yes," Chelsea told Sebastian, giving his hand a squeeze. "I would like that very much."

Chapter Five

I am not freaking out on the inside, Chelsea told herself as she walked hand in hand with Sebastian down the narrow path to the dock. *I am calm and collected, as if I go sneaking around late at night with hot random Brazilian guys I've just met all the time. This is utterly normal, and I am relaxed.*

Yeah. What a crock. Chelsea had the feeling that Sebastian could feel her hand sweating. She knew they weren't going somewhere quieter and more secluded just to talk. Sebastian was gorgeous and he was into her. Plus, he was pretty much the first guy to show interest in her since Pete Frasier in the seventh grade, who had kissed her once during spin the bottle and dribbled all over her chin. He had moved to Colorado the next year and sent her lovelorn e-mails until, presumably, he got over her and got on with his life. But Sebastian was *way* cuter than Pete Frasier: He had beautiful eyes and nice smooth skin and a sexy accent. Besides, Chelsea was tired of being the untouchable daughter-of-the-boss tomboy whom all the guys at the resort treated like a kid sister instead of a potentially datable girl. She wanted someone to see in her whatever it was that Todd saw in Vanessa that made him take her into the woods. She wanted someone to think she was hot.

"Uhm, want to sit in one of the boats?" Chelsea asked. There were no real seats on the dock, which was usually damp and slippery. Plus, maybe being on the water would calm her down a little.

"Whatever you'd like," Sebastian said. He climbed into the nearest motorboat, which had a wide vinyl backseat, then held out his hand to help Chelsea in as well. She almost laughed at the gesture—as *if* she couldn't get into a boat by herself!—but thought better of it. She recalled Leo helping Sara into the boat on the way to the party—why not enjoy a little princess treatment herself?

She slipped into the backseat next to Sebastian and turned off her headlamp, which she had been carrying as a flashlight. A milky, moonlit darkness enveloped them, and the sounds of the night seemed to sharpen: the faint beat of Yo La Tengo from the boom box up by the fire, a muffled shriek, an owl hooting, and the gentle *slap-slap* of the lake against the fiberglass sides of the boat.

Sebastian put his arm around her shoulders, and Chelsea slowly got used to its warmth and weight. She wasn't used to having a guy hold her like that, and it felt nice.

"I love it out here on the lake," she told Sebastian. "It really is my favorite place in the world."

"It's beautiful," he agreed. "Like you."

Chelsea couldn't help giggling at the cheesy line, and after a moment Sebastian joined her.

"I'm sorry," he apologized, keeping a hand on her shoulder as she shook with more giggles, gently rocking the boat so that it sent tiny ripples out over the water. "Give me a break—not everyone can be a bitter, sarcastic American like the teenagers on your TV shows."

"Like me," Chelsea said quietly.

"No, not like you," Sebastian replied earnestly, taking both her hands in his. "You're beautiful. And deep inside, you are passionate, too. I can see it in your eyes."

I think this is the part where we're supposed to kiss, Chelsea thought as Sebastian leaned in and placed his lips gently over hers. *And I think I'm supposed to close my eyes.*

She felt the beer buzzing inside her head as she relaxed in Sebastian's arms and let him kiss her. It was *nothing* like kissing Pete Frasier in the seventh grade. Sebastian's lips were soft and full, but firm underneath. Chelsea had never felt anything like this before. She nestled in closer to him, parting her lips just a little as he started taking tiny sips from her mouth. His hands massaged her back and roamed up to her neck, and one of them expertly removed the elastic on her ponytail while the other stroked her hair, starting from underneath where it met the nape of her neck and moving up to circle her ear, making her shiver against him.

She gently grabbed the back of his head and pulled him closer, not really knowing what she was doing and not really caring. All she knew was that whatever Sebastian was doing was not something she wanted to stop. She couldn't believe it: Here she was, hooking up with a boy she had just met! She pulled back a little so she could get another look at his face in the moonlight.

The back of her neck tingled where he had caressed it.

Sebastian tilted his head, grinning at her sweetly. Then his face seemed to brighten dramatically, as if it had been caught in the beam of a flashlight. Only then did Chelsea see the bobbing rays of light and hear the oddly familiar voices of the first wave of people approaching the docks, ready to turn in for the night.

"I think it's great that you guys come out here and do

this," a female voice was saying. "I'd love to see the island during the day."

Vanessa's sleek dark head was the first to pop out from the shadow of the trees, followed by Todd, Sara, and Leo. Chelsea immediately scooted out of Sebastian's arms and into the corner of the boat.

"Yeah, well, we'll keep 'em coming, hot and spicy, all summer long," Leo joked, mimicking a radio announcer.

Vanessa's burbling giggle spewed out over the lake, competing with Sara's mellow, silvery laugh. As they approached the boat, Chelsea had to shield her eyes against the bright glare coming from Todd's flashlight.

"Chelsea." Todd looked confused. "I was wondering where you'd gone off to. Didn't want to lose Daddy's little girl on her first night out." He laughed at his own joke and then paused, looking from her to Sebastian and then back again. "What are you doing?"

The same thing you were doing in the woods with Vanessa, Chelsea wanted to reply. But Sebastian stepped in for her.

"Chelsea was just showing me the boat," he told Todd.

"Yeah?" Todd cocked an eyebrow, and then he grinned. "She show you the dent where she hit it the first time she tried a one-eighty? I've never seen a human body slam into fiberglass that hard."

Everyone laughed, and Chelsea felt her cheeks go

scarlet. Did he really have to go there with all those other people around? Now she was more determined than ever to show him up this summer. She knew the only way she could put him in his place was by beating him at the Challenge. Just imagining it brightened her mood.

"If you look closely, there are a couple of Todd-induced scratches on this boat, too," she shot back. She felt a small surge of triumph as everyone else enjoyed a laugh at Todd's expense.

Todd scowled and changed the subject. "The girls got too cold, so we're heading back now," he said. "You guys coming with us or riding the next wave in?"

"Unfortunately, I have an early lesson tomorrow morning," Sebastian said. "Otherwise I would love to stay."

Todd climbed into the driver's seat, guiding Vanessa into the seat beside him, and started the engine before everyone else was even settled.

They went speeding across the lake so fast that Chelsea had to grab on to Sebastian to steady herself. "Todd, be careful!" she shouted toward him. "Don't overshoot the headlights!"

"Thanks, but I know how to drive one of these things," Todd sneered, nevertheless bringing the boat down to a safer speed. Chelsea couldn't help wondering what his deal was.

Todd drove with one hand on the wheel and used the other to hold on to Vanessa. Chelsea watched, a feeling rising in her chest, but then she felt Sebastian's hand slip stealthily around hers. "Thank you for, you know, showing me the boat," he whispered in her ear. A sweet, rushing feeling coursed through her body as their fingers intertwined in the darkness, and she gave him a tiny thank-you squeeze back.

Chapter Six

Stop horsing around back there!" Chelsea yelled from the back of the boat. She squinted out at the nine- and six-year-old McCullough brothers, who were each trying to jostle the other into the wake.

The boys paid no attention. For the past half hour, she had been trying to get them to take the sport seriously, but they were acting like the lake was a ball pit in a McDonald's playground. Mike rammed his body hard into Matt's side, sending his older brother sprawling into the chilly blue water.

"Ouch, you jerk!" Matt struggled to regain his footing and fell backward again as the boat hit a small rough patch.

"Ha-ha, dumbbell!" Mike stuck his tongue out at his

brother and suddenly lost his balance, plunging into the wake as well. "Aw, crap—that's cold."

"Stop the boat," Chelsea hissed to Nina, who obediently slowed down. Chelsea stood up on the back of the boat and grabbed the towrope for balance. "Okay, guys, get in here," she called to the McCullough boys, who continued to goof off as if they hadn't heard her. How did Todd manage to command so much respect from his students? All he had to do was raise an eyebrow and they jumped to follow his instructions.

"I mean it," Chelsea shouted to the boys from the boat, careful to keep herself steady. "It's time to come in. *Now!*"

The boys wailed in protest. "Do we *have* to?" Matt whined, bobbing up and down in the water.

"Right this second," Chelsea insisted. "Before I come out there and make you regret talking back to me."

Fear flashed in their eyes, and Matt was silent for once. Mike's lower lip began to tremble, and Chelsea immediately felt bad. She hadn't meant to be so harsh, but the boys were grating on her last remaining nerve. They swam awkwardly toward the boat, and Chelsea leaned down to fish them out of the water.

"Now listen," she firmly reprimanded them, a hand on each of their shoulders. "Wakeboarding is a privilege, okay? Your parents would rather I refund their money than bring home two mangled boys dumb enough to shove each other around a boat with a big powerful motor on it."

At that, Mike lost the battle for control of his lower lip and burst into tears. "I'm gonna be mangled, and it's all your fault!" he cried.

Matt shot Chelsea the evil eye. "Now look what you did," he snapped. "Mikey, it's okay. She doesn't know what she's talking about. . . . She's just being mean."

Chelsea sighed deeply. Teaching wakeboarding was way harder than she had anticipated. In the few days she'd been teaching, she was shocked by how bad people were at following instructions and paying attention. She just didn't get it. If people were shelling out so much money to learn to wakeboard, wouldn't they actually want to learn *how*? Yet nearly every lesson ended with her either clenching her teeth in frustration or fishing bedraggled would-be boarders out of the lake. It was beyond irritating, and Chelsea had nearly had enough. If this were an ordinary job, she might have considered quitting. But her father had trusted her with this. And she couldn't let him down over a few silly tourists. She could do this.

"Listen, I'm sorry." She awkwardly patted the still-weeping Mike McCullough's spiky wet hair. She glanced at her waterproof Fossil. "Hey, your lesson is almost over. Let's head back to shore, and I'll give you guys some coloring books that I have on water safety."

Matt sniffed. "We're too old for coloring books." Mike tugged on Matt's life vest and pulled him closer to whisper something in his ear. Matt rolled his eyes and addressed Chelsea again. "But I guess we'll take them anyway."

Chelsea nodded and turned her face away from them as Nina started the motor again and began to drive back to the dock. Chelsea watched the sunlight glint on the water's surface, refracting it into millions of tiny diamonds. It was a beautiful, clear day in the mountains, and she was not going to let one lousy morning lesson ruin it. She was just finding her inner calm when she felt a sharp, wet little poke on her arm and turned to see Matt prodding her.

"Yes?" She smiled, trying to hide her irritation.

"Do you have a boyfriend?" Matt looked up at her with large blue eyes that could almost be considered angelic . . . if she didn't know what a little devil he actually was.

The question caught Chelsea off guard—not only because it was inappropriate, but also because she didn't really know how to answer it. She remembered her first night with Sebastian, how they had kissed in the boat and he had held her hand all the way home. The day after the island party, Chelsea hadn't seen Sebastian until the staff gathered at their table in the far back corner of the giant high-ceilinged dining hall for dinner.

Her stomach had clenched so hard when she first looked into Sebastian's wide, dark eyes that she had nearly doubled over, but Sebastian just smiled as if they had a secret and he was happy about it. And that's exactly what he had said later that night, after catching up with her on the gravel path leading from the main lodge and walking with her down to the trees at the edge of the tennis courts.

"Are you sure you don't mind keeping this a secret for now?" Chelsea had asked. "Because—and I know this is going to sound weird, but—my parents are your bosses and, well . . ." She trailed off, unwilling to admit that she had never had a guy in her life for her parents to decide whether or not to disapprove of.

"It's fine," Sebastian had said, drawing her in closer to him for a long, deep kiss that left her breathless and shivering.

And that's how it had started. It had become almost a ritual over the past few days for him to slip discreetly out of the dining hall after dinner and wait for her around the corner of the lodge. Then they'd walk until they found somewhere secluded—a grove in the woods, the deserted dock over by the staff barracks, or the gear shed behind the tennis courts where nobody ever went at night. They would sink to the ground, barely touching the cool grass before attacking each other with their lips and hands. Sometimes they just lay together in the cool night air and talked as they looked up at the stars. Sebastian was easy to talk to: mellow, sweet, and full of stories about touring the world for tennis tournaments.

Chelsea went home each night and sneaked into bed feeling suffused in Sebastian, the sharp, sweet smell of his shampoo on her clothes and hands, the taste of his breath still in her mouth, and the imprint of his lips on her neck. She couldn't believe that, after years of watching all the other summer staffers hook up, she finally had a boy of her own. At the same time, she kept suppressing the nagging voice in the back of her head asking if Sebastian was really the *right* guy. Sure, he was handsome, sweet, and a really good kisser, but at times she felt like something was missing. If only she could figure out *what*.

"Hel-*loooo!*" Matt poked her several more times in the arm, jolting her back to her lesson on the lake. "*Chelseeeeeeea* . . . do you have a boyfriend or not? Because if not, Mikey wants to ask you out."

Matt dissolved into giggles as his little brother pummeled him to the boat's floor. Chelsea sighed and looked back out over the water.

*   *   *

Chelsea's stomach grumbled as she approached the lodge, and she realized that she'd missed lunch. She'd lingered too long in the shower after her lesson, trying to wash off Matt's comments and the jittery feeling that crept over her whenever she thought too much about her make-out sessions with Sebastian. She approached the dining hall and pushed through the heavy double doors that separated the grand, open dining space from the industrial kitchen. Opening one of the oversized fridges, she found several pans of leftover lasagna from the night before. She scooped a chunk onto one of the resort's earth-colored ceramic plates, popped it into the microwave, and leaned against the counter to relax until it was done.

She was thirty-four seconds away from a piping hot plate of lasagna when the doors swung open and Sara bustled into the kitchen, muttering to herself over a book she held open in her hand. She was clearly engrossed in whatever she was reading and paying so little attention to her surroundings that she banged her hip against a counter. Sara swore softly under her breath and hurried to the glass-doored beverage refrigerator, where she haphazardly removed a Vitamin Water.

Chelsea craned her neck to see what Sara was reading and realized it was a plant identification guide. Just then the microwave beeped. Sara yelped and nearly leapt out of her skin . . . dribbling purple Vitamin Water down the front of her white ruffled peasant blouse.

"Damn!" she cried. Looking up, she finally realized

that Chelsea was in the room, too, and Sara forced herself to smile—even though Chelsea could tell it was an effort. "Oh, hi, Chels," she said absently, looking down at the stain as if she could will it away with her glare.

"Are you okay?" Chelsea asked, scrambling to get some paper towels from over the sink. This was the first time she'd ever seen Sara get flustered. It was strangely refreshing.

"Oh yeah, I'm fine." Sara grimaced as she dabbed at the growing purple splotch on her shirt.

"You sure?"

"It's just . . . well, I'm giving my first nature walk in half an hour, and I had that outfit planned for the past week. Now I have to go find something else because my shirt is ruined," Sara admitted. "I should go change."

"Do you want me to go back to the house with you?" Chelsea offered. Normally she wouldn't have, but Sara was acting like such a basket case that without supervision Chelsea was afraid that she would just put on the same shirt, only backward and inside out, and then probably tell Chelsea's parents that it had all been their daughter's fault.

"Yeah!" Sara brightened. "That would be great."

Gulping down her lasagna in two bites, Chelsea put the dirty plate in the sink and followed Sara out the doors of the kitchen, through the empty dining room, and into the bright afternoon sunlight.

"I can't believe you're so nervous," she said to Sara as they hurried up the path to their house.

"Oh, I hate public speaking," Sara admitted. "Half the time I get so nervous, I nearly throw up beforehand."

"You seem like such a natural," Chelsea said. "The way you spoke at the orientation and stuff."

Sara laughed. "I'm guess I'm a good actress," she said.

They reached the house, and the girls hurried upstairs. Sara went into her room and Chelsea hovered at the door, wondering if she should disappear into her own bedroom, but Sara motioned her inside. "Come on, I need your help," she begged. "What do you think . . . does this look okay?" She pulled a soft cotton American Apparel wrap dress with thin lavender stripes from her closet and frowned.

"It's nice," Chelsea said, feeling awkward that Sara was asking her for fashion advice. Had she not noticed that Chelsea basically lived in wetsuits and track pants?

"Yeah . . . ," Sara said skeptically. "Yeah, but too girly. I need something more authoritative and better for hiking."

She rummaged in her closet and came up with a cream-colored button-down shirt with a green fern print from Banana Republic.

"I like it," Chelsea said. "The leaves are perfect for a nature walk."

"Yeah?" Sara slipped off her ruined blouse and tossed it in the corner of the room, pulling on the new shirt and buttoning it up, leaving it just a little open around her neck. She twirled around so Chelsea could get a better look. "What do you think?"

A stab of jealousy shot through Chelsea when she saw how good Sara looked. The blouse hugged her curves, showing and hiding skin in just the right places, her tan radiant against the cream-colored fabric. Even though Sara had planned her whole outfit, the blouse swapped in perfectly to match her dark trouser jeans and brown leather sandals. "You look great," Chelsea admitted, looking down at her own shorts and flip-flops, which suddenly seemed very boring.

Sara acted unusually happy with Chelsea's answer. "I'm so glad!" she chirped. "I haven't even worn this yet, but I knew it would come in handy sometime."

"Oh. Yeah," Chelsea said dubiously. She bought only clothes that were super-comfortable, and that she knew she would actually wear.

"Okay, almost showtime," Sara murmured, probably more to herself than Chelsea. She suddenly looked nervous again, as she took a couple of small sips from her Vitamin Water. "You're coming, right?"

Chelsea had actually been planning to go wakeboarding instead, but Sara was looking at her so expectantly that she couldn't think of a way out.

She followed Sara's brisk stride to the meeting point by the lake, and Chelsea couldn't help being worried for her. She knew the Glitterlake Resort summer tourist crowd pretty well—well enough to know that the *last* thing they'd want to do on a balmy Saturday afternoon in the recreation capital of Northern California was take two hours to go on a nature hike and learn how to identify plants. Tourists around Tahoe liked action, partying, and spending money, and that translated into sports, nightlife, and gambling. Nature walks just didn't fit into the equation, and even though Chelsea wasn't crazy about her half sister's sudden and unexpected intrusion into her life, she wasn't looking forward to watching her learn all of this the hard way.

The girls rounded the bend leading up to the trailhead of the small, seldom-used two-mile hiking trail that wound its way around the resort's property. Chelsea stopped, shocked when she saw a crowd of at least thirty people. She picked out her mother and father immediately, and a few of the elderly couples and families staying at the resort. But the biggest surprise was the sheer number of guys in their late teens and early twenties who had, apparently overnight, developed a rampant curiosity about plant identification. Amongst them she spotted Tim, Joel, Ted, Leo, and—Chelsea couldn't believe it—Todd. The glare of the sunlight was pretty bright, but Chelsea would recognize that thick dirty-blond hair and those piercing lake-colored eyes anywhere.

The crowd of guys broke into spontaneous applause and whistles when Sara approached. As she headed toward the front of the crowd, Sara's shoulders straightened and her walk became more purposeful. By the time she turned to face them, every trace of the anxiety was gone from her face. She smiled and waved.

"Thank you all so much for coming to the first *ever* Glitterlake Resort Plant and Tree Identification Walk!" she said enthusiastically. "I'm so glad you could make it. Now, I hope you all wore comfortable shoes and brought water, because . . ."

Sara launched into a laundry list of safety precautions, and Chelsea wandered over to join her parents at the back of the crowd. They beamed at Sara with what Chelsea could have sworn was even more pride than when she had won her first wakeboarding trophy at the Tahoe Junior Invitational.

"How's it going, Champ?" Chelsea's dad asked, putting his arm around her shoulders. "Teaching going okay?"

"Oh yeah. It's just great!" Chelsea said, plastering a somewhat fake smile on her face. For once, she couldn't say anything to him—not about the party or Sebastian and certainly not about how badly she was doing with the McCullough boys.

"Good. I knew you'd be great. There's nothing you can't do if you set your mind to it, Chels." Chelsea looked up and saw the proud look on her dad's face and felt like she would burst into tears.

"Sara seems to be doing well so far," Chelsea began, trying to change the subject.

"I know! Isn't this exciting?" Her mom grabbed her hand and squeezed it tightly as Sara informed everyone that they were all standing under a giant ponderosa pine. "I had no idea these walks would be so popular."

"We should have thought of doing them years ago," her dad agreed. "I don't know why we didn't."

Up front, Sara motioned for everyone to follow her, and the group snaked slowly along the path. The cadre of boys up front jostled one another to get closer to Sara as the few kids who had tagged along rushed around their legs to exclaim over the jack-in-the-pulpit Sara was pointing out.

"She is an absolute natural," Chelsea's mom said proudly. "And she just looks lovely in that blouse."

Chelsea tugged at her ratty old tee and wondered if her mom was ashamed of the way she dressed. It hadn't really occurred to her before, but maybe her mom wished she would wear prettier things—stuff like Sara's. Chelsea hung back, trying to think of how to bring this up with her mom without making it into a big deal.

But her mom was already rushing ahead to look at

some purple blossoms that Sara had discovered by the side of the path. Chelsea wondered if she should just turn around and go home. But at that very moment, Todd hung back and tried to strike up a conversation.

"Hey, Chels. What's up?" He sauntered up to her with his thumbs hooked casually in the belt loops of his cargo shorts. He flashed his adorable lopsided smile, and Chelsea's heart began thrumming like the motor in an idling boat. She'd managed to avoid him pretty well since the island party and had thought she was making progress on the whole getting-over-it thing.

"Not much," she whispered—because she didn't want to interrupt Sara's plant talk, of course, and *not* because standing this close to Todd made her lose her voice. Definitely not.

"Your sister sure knows her stuff, huh?" Todd said. "Pretty impressive."

Chelsea's cheeks went hot and her palms started to sweat at the same time. She was so sick of hearing about how great Sara was that she could have screamed. It wasn't like plant walks were a competitive sport or anything—nobody had ever won a medal giving tours. It wasn't even high-risk. The way Chelsea saw it, they were just a random pastime . . . and one of Sara's many ways to look cute and be on display. "Yeah, you just try getting her on a wakeboard and see how she does then."

"Good idea," Todd said, grinning. "I just might do

that." And he wandered back into the crowd, leaving Chelsea to fume by herself in the rear of the group.

The thought of Sara trying to learn wakeboarding made her skin crawl. But the thought of her learning from Todd was even worse. Wakeboarding was the one thing that Chelsea had left, the one area where she would always be better than Sara. She fervently hoped that Todd wasn't serious—if so, it was almost like he was doing it just to hurt her. Chelsea might have been a strong, kick-ass chick on a wakeboard, but that obviously didn't extend to matters of the heart.

Chapter Seven

What's so great about Sara anyway? Chelsea asked herself as she trudged along the path home. So she knew a lot about plants—Eugene Fitzgibbon from Chelsea's freshman biology class had known a lot about invertebrates, and it wasn't like the whole world went falling all over the place over *him*. Usually knowing a lot about something dorky like plants was a good way to get people to make fun of you, not act like you were the coolest thing to happen to Glitterlake Resort since Todd showed up to start the water sports program. *Todd.* Chelsea sighed.

Deep down Chelsea knew that the way people reacted to Sara had *nothing* to do with her expertise in local flora. People liked Sara because she was nice, and laughed a lot, and always had fun. But mostly, people (especially guys) liked Sara because she was pretty, and well-dressed, and acted like . . . well, like a girl.

Chelsea unlocked the door to her house and climbed the stairs to her room. Nobody ever came right out and said that being good at all that girly stuff was what made guys really like you, but that was obviously the way it was. Between her experience with the girly girls at school and now her sister, Chelsea felt like she stuck out like an overgrown third-grader.

She plopped down on the end of her bed. It was probably only a matter of time before Sebastian, too, would see that she was a sporty, competitive, too-tall tomboy and lose all interest. What did he see in her anyway?

After tossing and turning and generally wallowing in frustration for about as long as she could take it, Chelsea decided to go wakeboarding after all. She knew it would make her feel better to get in a solid hour before dinner.

But as she passed Sara's room, she saw the stained shirt that Sara had discarded on the floor before the plant walk through the open door. And beyond that Chelsea could see her closet, with the doors wide open showing beautiful, feminine summer clothes made out of silk and linen and soft brushed Egyptian cotton. Chelsea couldn't even imagine the expense that had gone into amassing that wardrobe, let alone the hours and hours of shopping and trying on clothes that must have accompanied it. Most of her own clothing came from stores and Web sites that also sold things like carabineers, tennis rackets, and surf wax.

So she couldn't quite understand why she was suddenly entering Sara's room, gliding over to the closet, and running her hands along the rows of skirts, blouses, and sundresses. Or why her hand lingered on a flimsy silk shirt the exact color of the lake first thing in the morning, rubbing the tissue-papery sleeve between her fingers. Or why she took the blouse off the hanger and held it up against herself, the fabric cool and light against her bare arms.

Chelsea was usually fairly aware of her motivations for doing things, but she couldn't quite explain what drew her to slip the shirt on over her lime green Roxy tank top with the built-in bra—or why, when she saw the way she looked in the mirror, all she could do was stand there staring at the way it seemed to soften her features and bring out the blue in her eyes.

The thud of footsteps coming up the stairs jolted Chelsea out of her trance. She quickly stashed the top back in the closet and practically leapt out of the room. Sara was coming down the hall.

"Did you need something?" Sara asked her.

"No, thanks, I'm good," Chelsea stuttered. Then she pushed past Sara, down the stairs, and out the door. She ran along the paths connecting the buildings, her breath settling into a regular rhythm. Her Pumas crunched against the gravel, and beads of sweat started to pop out on her forehead. What had she been thinking, snooping around like that? Since when did Chelsea care about clothes? She felt stupid and clueless, like she just wasn't herself anymore.

Chelsea ran past several honeymooning couples and a few families straggling back up from the resort's private beach, dragging towels, half-empty sodas, and industrial-sized bottles of sunscreen. She even passed the McCullough family and ignored Matt completely when he yelled after her, "Where ya goin', Chels? To meet your *boyfriend*?"

Where am I going? That was a good question. And then she realized she was running down to the lake. For her, the lake had magical healing properties. Whenever she was on the water, her troubles fell away and she could finally be at peace.

As she reached the dock, she slowed down to a jog, wondering if she should take out one of the boats and give herself some real peace and quiet. That's when she saw Todd, tying off a boat as he said good-bye to a middle-aged guy whose wetsuit stretched thin around his sizable paunch. The man was thanking him for a great lesson. "You're a real slave driver and you're harsh, man, but you're the best coach I ever had," the man was saying, standing so close to Todd that his hair dripped onto Todd's Chaco sandals. "You sure know how to whip a guy into shape. Think you got time for another lesson tomorrow?"

"Maybe. You can check with the front desk for my schedule," Todd said, shooting the man his twenty-million-dollar grin as he shook his hand. The guy walked off to the locker room, briefly smiling at Chelsea as he passed. Looking after him, Todd noticed Chelsea and waved. She wondered if she should have turned around, but it was too late now.

"Hey, want to take the boat out?" Todd asked. "I'm dying to ride. And it looks like you are, too." He always seemed to read her mind, though she could never read his.

Chelsea was annoyed that her emotion showed so obviously on her face, but the thought was beyond tempting. Landing the whirlybird 540 she'd been working on for the past week would make up for all the weird things that had happened that day, and Chelsea was aching to give it another shot. Even if it meant being around Todd.

"Definitely," she said, heading toward the locker room on the side of the boathouse where the staff kept their gear. "Just let me change."

Chelsea slipped into her wetsuit in the comforting dankness of the locker room and started to feel better.

The embarrassing incident with Sara still lingered in the back of her mind: She really hadn't meant to sneak into Sara's room—it felt strange. But all of that was now eclipsed with the delicious, tingling anticipation of a long late-afternoon ride on the lake with Todd.

His sexy lopsided grin met her as she emerged from the boathouse, and Chelsea was floored. Was it possible that his biceps had gotten even more defined in the week since he'd arrived at the resort? His hair was certainly lighter and his tan darker from being out on the water all day. He climbed into the driver's seat and started the engine, and she hurried to toss her board in beside him and untie the rope that tethered the boat to the shore.

"So, Chels." Todd maneuvered the boat into the open water, his hand loose on the throttle.

"So, Todd," Chelsea mimicked flirtatiously, feelings rising and falling in her chest. Being with him felt so right and natural, and at the same time very awkward and wrong.

"Do you really think Sara would be into learning how to wakeboard?" he continued.

The beginnings of Chelsea's buoyant mood deflated. "How would I know?" she snapped.

Todd shot her a quizzical look from under his thick eyebrows. "I dunno—maybe because she's your sister?"

"Half," Chelsea corrected.

But Todd just shrugged. "Wow, you're testy," he observed. "Get out of the boat and into the lake before you bite my head off."

He was right. The only thing that could make her happy at this point was landing that damn jump. Chelsea grabbed her board, slid her goggles on over her eyes, and leapt off the back of the boat, letting the towrope go taut in her hands as she stood on the board.

The nothing-else-matters feeling washed over her the moment the delicious flying sensation kicked in, and she laughed into the wind. *Oh yeah. Wakeboarding is good.* No matter what else happened, she would always have this.

She warmed up with a few simple handle passes in and out of the wake and built up to a couple of 180-degree jumps and spins that had her body buzzing and her brain focused 100 percent. She realized she would work things out with Sara somehow. And Sebastian, too. He was a good guy.

Chelsea flung herself into a 360-degree flat-line spin, rotating her body over the rope and landing on her feet, laughing into a face full of foamy spray.

She thought she could see Todd raise his eyes in surprise in the rearview mirror, but she couldn't be sure from eighty feet away. Well, if he thought that was impressive, she would show *him*. She took a huge, clarifying breath as she built up her momentum. Chelsea navigated way outside the wake and then gathered speed coming back in. She bent her knees deeply and launched her body high into the air. She rotated for half a turn, then a full one and then, *for the first time ever*, she completed another half turn before the lake rushed up toward her. She made a quick save and planted her feet. *Yes!* She landed triumphantly in the calm center of the wake and did a quick 180 handle pass so that she was facing the boat again. This time there was no mistaking Todd's look of awed reverence in the mirror . . . even from the full eighty feet away. Chelsea pumped her left fist above her head, yelling, "Hell, yeah!" in her best I-rock-the-world battle cry. Then, exhausted but elated, she maneuvered her way up the towrope.

"I can't believe you landed that jump!" Todd said excitedly when she climbed back into the boat wet and triumphant.

"Why?" Chelsea grinned as she squeezed out her ponytail. "Didn't think I had it in me?"

Todd sapphire eyes flickered. Was that doubt, envy, or something else entirely? As familiar as Chelsea was with how his body moved, with all those summers spent together on the lake, she could never seem to read his mind. But she wasn't going to let it get her down: not after landing that whirlybird 540!

"Eh, you're just having a good run." Todd zipped up his wetsuit and got ready to go out on the water.

"Whatever," she laughed. "Let's see what you can do," she said, reaching out to tousle his hair–without even thinking about it. His hair was surprisingly soft and fine between her fingers.

"Well, your handle pass at the end was a little sloppy," Todd said sulkily.

"Let's see if you can top it then, champ." Chelsea reached over and tousled his hair one more time. Just because it felt too good not to.

Chapter Eight

Chelsea was high on life during dinner that night. She'd landed her best jump to date. Todd was jealous. It was exactly what she wanted. Well, that and maybe to feel his soft hair in her fingers just once more. As she chewed the last of her broccoli, she felt something nudge her foot. Sebastian, who'd sat down across from her, was apparently trying to play footsie with her. She smiled at him but felt weird. They were in the *dining hall*—not exactly a turn-on. Plus, anyone might see. He was chatting with Sienna, who sat to his left, but he kept looking at Chelsea.

As soon as she finished her frozen yogurt, Sebastian gave her a sly wink from across the table before he got up to leave. She knew what *that* meant. Twenty minutes later they were on the cool grass behind the tennis shed and Chelsea was sighing softly as Sebastian's expert tongue circled her ear.

"You're so beautiful," he whispered before moving down to plant a series of soft, slow kisses on her neck. She closed her eyes and ran her hands through his hair, which, despite the clean, soapy scent that had become so familiar to her, was surprisingly rough and dry compared with Todd's.

Stop thinking about Todd! she commanded herself. *You're kissing Sebastian—who happens to be a total hottie, in case you haven't noticed.*

Still, she couldn't strike the image of Todd in the middle of the water, his jaw squared and his hair fluttering in the wind as he straddled the wake.

Thinking about Todd while she was making out with Sebastian felt weird, but once she started, it was hard to make herself stop. Why did he have to look so good but act so distant? Was he as good a kisser as Sebastian? Maybe he was even better.

"What's wrong?" Sebastian removed his hand from around her waist and lay back on the grass, grasping her hand in his.

"Nothing!" Chelsea exclaimed. "Where'd you go?" Chelsea leaned over, trying to get them kissing again.

"I don't know," Sebastian said, resisting. "You seem a little . . . preoccupied."

Chelsea thought about all the things that *had* been preoccupying her: how she had made Mikey McCullough cry, Sara's clothes, and the boat ride with Todd.

"Let me guess," Sebastian said, playing with her hand. "You're jealous because Sara is getting so much attention, and you feel like you can't live up."

"What?" Chelsea yelped. Was that how it looked? She didn't feel like going into it with Sebastian. She would rather be making out.

"Is being a teacher harder than you thought?" Sebastian prodded. He was hitting all her sore points.

"That's mainly it," she said, relieved to finally be talking to someone—even if it was only about *one* of her problems. "I had these two boys today and . . . well, I made one of them cry."

"Ouch," Sebastian said. "Do you think you're being too hard on them?"

"I was just trying to help!" Chelsea protested. "You wouldn't believe what murder these kids are. They won't listen to anything I say. I'm trying to teach them, but my butt is on the line if they get hurt."

"Just don't freak out about it so much." Sebastian moved closer to her. He took her into his arms and started smoothing her hair. "If you make it fun, they'll be on your side."

"Thanks. I know," Chelsea muttered. She couldn't

imagine ever actually being on Matt McCullough's side. Nor could she figure out how to make the boys annoy her less so she could even *think* about how to make things fun. She broke away from Sebastian's caress and turned over to face him, giving him a weak smile. "Now, enough talking." She reached for him again and lost herself in the blissful feeling of his lips. Sebastian pulled her down on top of him, and Chelsea prayed that he wouldn't stop again.

Chapter Nine

You don't need to be so scared of the water," Chelsea urged Britney, the sweet-tempered twelve-year-old who was that morning's wakeboarding lesson. Chelsea chuckled a little at how different Britney was from the McCullough brothers she'd had the day before. "All you have to do is go out there, keep your feet on the board, your knees bent, and hold on to the rope."

"But what if I fall?" Britney's big brown eyes widened with worry.

"You're not going to drown," Chelsea assured her. "You have a life vest on, remember?"

"Are you sure I'll be okay?" Britney asked.

"I promise," Chelsea assured her. "I wouldn't let you go out there if something was going to happen to you."

"But my bindings feel loose. . . ."

Chelsea sighed again as she leaned down to look at the bindings on Britney's rented board. She frowned. The bindings were as tight as they'd go. "They look fine to me," she assured Britney. "Why don't you just give it a try, okay?"

"All right." But Britney still sounded dubious. Chelsea helped her out of the boat, calling after her to crouch down low until she was sure she had her balance. She wasn't even positive that Britney heard her as she paddled out until the rope was slack.

"All right, now crouch low, low, low, and then stand up and turn around!" Chelsea screamed over the noise of the boat's motor. Britney looked panicked. Her head bobbed up and down in the wake as she struggled to hang on to the towrope. She screamed something, but Chelsea couldn't hear her.

"What, Britney?" Chelsea yelled. The little girl hollered something incoherent again as she struggled in the water.

"Just get your weight on top of the board!" Chelsea called.

"I can't do it!" Britney wailed, very loudly and clearly this time.

Exasperated, Chelsea jumped off the side of the boat and paddled out to where Britney was floating in the water. "All right, I'm here," she said. "Now, I'm going to hold on to you and I want you to focus on getting all of your weight on the board."

"Noooo, I can't do it!" Britney sputtered again helplessly.

"Just try it one more time." Chelsea tried to sound calming. "We're going to do the exact same thing, only this time don't lean forward so much. Are you ready?" She put her hands back on Britney's waist.

"No!" Britney said, wriggling free. "I want to go back on the boat."

"Come on, one more time," Chelsea coaxed. "Don't be a quitter, Brit. Give it another shot, okay?"

"I am *not* a quitter!" Britney insisted, treading water.

"Then try one more time."

"All right," Britney said. But she didn't look happy about it. Not one bit.

Chelsea squinted in the bright sunlight and moved in toward her again. She put her hands on Britney's waist and counted off. "One, two, three, go!" Chelsea said, a little gentler this time.

This time, instead of pitching forward, Britney leaned back too far and plopped backward into the wake on her butt.

"That's it!" she screamed when she resurfaced. "I don't want to do this anymore. Let me get back in the boat or I'll tell my dad you kept me out here and he'll sue you for reckless endangerment."

"Okay, fine," Chelsea said. Since when did twelve-year-olds know so much about lawsuits and reckless endangerment? She swam back to the boat with Britney and helped her climb in, even wrapping a towel around her shoulders.

"You seemed a little scared out there," she observed as they headed back to shore. She meant to sound sympathetic, but Britney took offense.

"I was *not*," she insisted. "You just pushed me before I was ready."

"But learning to get up is the very first thing you need to figure out when you start wakeboarding," Chelsea explained. She remembered how easily she had gotten it the first time. Todd had taken her out on the boat, explained the basics, and told her to keep her weight balanced. After just two tries, she was standing up in the wake, laughing into the wind. Within days she was cutting back and forth across the wake, and after a month of almost daily practice she was getting air on most of her jumps and learning basic handle passes. It had been so easy for her—her body had taken to the sport almost immediately, and as soon as she tried it, she hadn't wanted to do anything else. As much as she wanted to empathize with Britney, she just couldn't understand why it would be so hard—or so scary. "You just have to keep trying."

"Well, I'm never going to get it if you keep pushing me so hard," Britney grumbled.

"I'm sorry, Brit," Chelsea said. Should she admit that she was new to this whole teaching thing and still learning the ropes? She didn't want Britney to report back to her parents—who had rented one of the deluxe cabins complete with fireplace and private outdoor Jacuzzi—that Glitterlake hired amateurs. "We'll take it easier next time, okay?"

"If there even *is* a next time." Britney turned away and stuck her nose in the air.

*   *   *

Chelsea chewed her grilled Swiss-and-tomato sandwich and glanced around the lunch table, where most of the summer staffers continued to linger over big glasses of iced tea, sharing irate-vacationer war stories.

"So, dude, get this one," Leo said as he leaned back in his chair. "I'm slinging brews up at Snowmass late one Saturday night . . . about to close up shop and starting to chase everyone out. There's this couple over in the corner playing darts—been there all night, drinking beers and shots of JD, tipping well. But I guess they got in an argument or something—honestly, I didn't even see, I was cashing out—'cause next thing I know, the guy comes over to me and he's got a dart sticking out of his head."

The entire table laughed and some of the girls giggled.

"No shit," Leo continued. "Right there in the outside corner of his left eye. And I'm like, 'Uh, you okay, man? You want me to call 911?' And the guy's just standing there like he's trying to think what to say next. So I take him down to the ER and they're all freaking out trying to get an eye specialist in, when the orderly who was supposed to prep him comes out holding the dart in his hand. The guy is fine—it missed the nerve by, like, millimeters. The next day I saw him out on the slopes." Leo shrugged amidst a chorus of guffaws of protest. Chelsea glanced over at Sara, who was smiling at Leo and shaking her head in disbelief. As usual, she looked like she'd just stepped out of the pages of *Teen Vogue*. Her hair was swept back in a tight bun that made her cheekbones stand out, and she wore a plaid Ben Sherman dress offset by a simple pearl necklace and matching earrings. It was a cute, preppy look that Chelsea could never have pulled off in a million years. Everything about Sara seemed to sparkle: her eyes, her skin, even her laugh. No wonder everyone thought she was so great. Too bad the only sparkling Chelsea ever did was behind a boat.

Chelsea suddenly realized that everyone at the table was looking at her expectantly.

"So what do you think, Chels?" Leo asked.

"Huh?" Chelsea felt ridiculous with so many eyes on her.

"Hello—what have we just been talking about for the

past ten minutes?" Nina joked. "Earth to Chelsea . . . the party?"

"Party?" Chelsea's ears perked up. If she was getting invited to yet another staff party, she was definitely making progress.

"*Pool* party," Leo corrected. "Soft lighting, cold beers, hot chicks in bikinis"—he glanced sideways at Sara, then quickly gave Chelsea a winning grin—"unprecedented fun in the spa building. What do you think?"

"I don't know." Chelsea was sure that if her parents found out about a party like that, they'd be furious. She had always suspected that they knew about the island parties but turned a blind eye because they weren't on the resort's property and didn't affect business. But the spa building . . . that was only about a five-minute walk from the main lodge. Plus, it was state-of-the-art, designed by a famous architect, and had been really expensive to build. Chelsea knew that her parents had needed to take out a bank loan just to fund the embedded speakers and underwater lighting. She certainly didn't *want* to say no to the other staffers, but . . . her dad would never forgive her if something happened.

"We totally won't trash the place," Mel said, as if reading her mind. "I mean, come on, I work there—I care about keeping it clean as much as you do!"

"And we'll only drink out of plastic cups so we don't

have to worry about broken glass," Leo assured her. "I'll even run the bar if you want."

Chelsea looked around the table at all the summer staffers staring at her expectantly. She knew the decision was up to her—she was the only one who knew where her parents kept the keys to the building.

"I think it's a lame idea," a low voice said from down the table. Chelsea turned toward it and found herself looking straight into Todd's eyes. "Why would we want to hang by the pool when there's a lake right there? Besides, Little McCormick would never do something that could get her in trouble." He had his signature smug grin as he looked at Chelsea.

Chelsea's face flushed with humiliation and anger. "Well, I think it's an amazing idea," she said. "Let's do it on Sunday night, after the Fourth of July weekend when tourists have gone home." She couldn't believe she had just said yes. But there was no way she was going to let Todd get the best of her in front of everyone.

A round of cheers broke out, and Sebastian gave Chelsea's knee a more-than-friendly squeeze under the table. Todd shrugged, lifted his tray, and walked off.

*   *   *

Chelsea went into her bedroom after lunch and lay down on the bed, looking up at the posters she'd plastered to the walls, showing her favorite pro wake-boarders suspended in the air in the midst of tricks she dreamed of mastering someday. But for once, boarding wasn't the first thing on her mind. Instead, her thoughts were a jumble of anxiety over the pool party, confusion over what was going on with Sebastian, and jealousy over how easy Sara seemed to have it and how well everyone treated her.

Maybe the pool party would be her chance to show the world that she could be as girly and feminine as Sara after all. Chelsea went to her swimsuit drawer and rifled through its contents: one-piece practice Speedos, lots of board shorts, and one navy blue tankini—which, she realized to her dismay, was the sexiest piece of swimwear she owned. Even though it showed off only a tiny sliver of stomach and practically came up to her collarbone.

She heard Sara's footsteps descending the stairs and then the front door swing shut behind her, followed by a long wash of silence. Chelsea's parents were probably up at the main lodge, and if Sara really planned to hike the ponderosa trail like she'd told Chelsea she was going to on the way back to their house, she'd be gone for a good long time.

This is for research purposes only, Chelsea said to herself as she opened the door to Sara's room and headed toward her closet. And this time, she'd pay attention.

Chapter Ten

Could they have picked a nicer day to hold the Fourth of July on?" Leo joked, standing on the top of the ladder as he stood to hang red, white, and blue bunting along the deck. "Hey, do me a favor and refill this staple gun, would you?"

"No problem." Chelsea dug around in the toolbox and slipped a row of industrial staples into the staple gun, handing it back up to Leo along with more bunting. Looking out over the tops of the guest cabins and the red clay tennis courts to the lake, she had to agree with Leo. It was a balmy seventy-eight degrees, and the sun shone cheerfully overhead, warming her shoulders as a light breeze rippled the lake's sparkling surface.

"Oh, the deck looks wonderful!" Chelsea's mom called over. Patty slipped through the double-glass doors with her cell phone in one hand and a big sheaf of papers in the other. She was clearly in a hurry to get down to the delivery dock around the side of the building and greet the pyrotechnicians who had come to set up the fireworks, but she still stopped to give Chelsea a kiss on the cheek before hurrying down the wooden stairs.

The sweet gesture made Chelsea happy, but that was quickly shot through with a cold prickle of guilt. Earlier that day, while her parents were doing their daily inspections of the guest cabins and outbuildings, she had sneaked into their office and slipped the spare set of spa keys into her pocket.

She watched as her mom's back disappeared down the stairs; then she pulled the key out of her pocket and handed it to Leo.

"Thanks!" Leo said, giving her a conspiratorial wink. "And don't worry about a thing. I have it all under control."

Chelsea laughed nervously. She knew she could trust Leo, but she was still a little afraid. "You know, if we get caught—," she began.

"Hey, relax. Everything will be okay," Leo said easily, squeezing Chelsea's shoulder. "It's all good."

"What's all good?" Sienna hurried up the stairs with Mel right behind her.

"Sorry, can't tell you," Leo laughed from atop the ladder. "Top secret."

"Ooooooh," Mel breathed. "I know what *this* is about." She leaned in toward Chelsea and whispered in her ear. "Thanks for doing this, Chels! It's going to be great."

Chelsea's cheeks warmed at Mel's excitement. It was the first time she had ever felt really included by the other staffers. While they had always been perfectly nice, Chelsea was used to feeling like the staff was a popular clique that could never really include her—and that Mel and Sienna were its ringleaders.

"Good times." Sienna absentmindedly air-kissed both Chelsea's cheeks before hurrying inside.

"Well, Chelsea, I think we're all done." Leo climbed down the ladder with the staple gun balanced in one hand.

"You sure?" Chelsea asked.

"Positive," Leo assured her. "I'm gonna go find your sister and see if she'll give me a hand with the American flag window decals."

Chelsea almost reminded him that Sara was her *half* sister, but at the last minute decided not to. It was too beautiful a day, and she was in too good a mood.

*   *   *

Chelsea thought she could really get the hang of the whole skirt thing as she made her way from her family's house down to the barbecue area on the lake. In honor of the special occasion, the day's unusually balmy weather, and her new commitment to dressing more feminine, Chelsea was wearing a knee-length maroon skirt she had borrowed from Sara's closet in another weird hot-clothes-induced trance. She'd meant to tell Sara about it, and apologize and offer to return it, but she had been so busy, she just hadn't gotten around to it. She figured Sara owned so many clothes that she probably wouldn't even notice—and if she did, Chelsea could always just say she owned the same one.

"Chelsea, you look totally cute!" Mel exclaimed, greeting her with a hug when she arrived at the barbecue area. Chelsea flushed with pride. She had paired the skirt with one of her cuter tank tops and even pulled it all together with a pretty but simple pair of dangly gold earrings from H&M. "I don't think I've ever seen you wear a skirt before. And that's a great tank top—you have amazing shoulders!"

"Thanks." Chelsea smiled, embarrassed but pleased at the compliment. She looked around: The nearby tables and lawn were swarming with summer staffers and tourists scarfing perfectly grilled burgers and salmon steaks and drinking freshly chilled Sierra Nevadas. "Are those burgers as good as they look?"

"Delicious," Mel laughed. "Go get one!"

Chelsea wove through the crowd toward the big gas

grill that she knew was her father's pride and joy. He stood behind it, brandishing a spatula and grinning through the rising smoke.

"Medium rare for my favorite Champ?" he asked jovially, flipping burgers as he talked. "Grab a bun."

Seeing her dad in such a good mood made Chelsea grin. She grabbed a plate from the long buffet table next to the grill and piled it high with potato salad and a big slice of watermelon. When she looked up, she saw Todd standing directly across the table from her, giving her a strange look.

"What?" she challenged.

"Nothing," he shot back. "You're just . . . Well, forget it."

"I'm just *what?*" she asked, not wanting him to saunter off and leave her to spend the rest of the day wondering what he had been thinking. She was sick of always wishing she knew what was on his mind.

"You look different," Todd observed. "Did you do something to your hair?"

Chelsea couldn't help laughing. "Nope," she said.

Todd looked her up and down. "It must be the glow of knowing you're about to do something stupid."

"What?" Chelsea demanded. Was he referring to the pool party? Couldn't he just let her have a good time like everyone else?

"I mean—that," he answered, pointing at her knee.

She looked down to where a blob of ketchup had dripped from her burger and landed on the corner of her skirt. *Sara's* skirt. *Crap.*

"Good luck with that, Little M," Todd chuckled, turning toward the tables.

Chelsea quickly rotated the skirt so the stain was hidden on the back, and hurried to catch up with him.

"Chelsea, Todd, hey!" A happy chorus went up when they arrived at the picnic table and sat down. Sebastian hadn't shown up yet, and she briefly wondered where he was. As Chelsea bit into her burger, the staffers began to talk excitedly about the gorgeous weather, the myriad of tourists, and of course, the secret pool party.

"What do you think, Chels, do you want to bring CDs or just trust Leo's iPod?" Sienna asked.

"Hey, what's wrong with my iPod?" Leo demanded.

"Oh, I dunno, it's probably all emo," Sienna joked.

Leo pretended to be insulted. "Uhm, hello . . . *and Primus.*"

Chelsea tuned out as they bantered back and forth. Despite Todd's teasing her, the feeling she'd gotten earlier that day of being truly included for the first time ever had come back, and she let herself soak in it like a nice, warm bath. It felt so good to belong.

"I'm going to go get some dessert." She started toward the buffet table and piled her plate with strawberry cheesecake. As she was headed back toward the staff table, she heard her mother's voice and turned her head to see her sitting on a picnic blanket, head-to-head with Sara. Chelsea was closer to her dad than her mom, but it still bothered her to see her mom and Sara getting along so well and having so much fun together—almost as if they were friends instead of daughter and stepmom. Wasn't it obvious how Sara was just trying to worm her way into their family?

"Boo!" Sebastian slipped his arm around her shoulders. "Sorry it took me so long to get here—had to finish a long lesson. The fireworks are starting soon. Want to watch with me?"

"Okay," Chelsea agreed. She was sorry that she couldn't go back and hang out with Todd and the others, but it made her feel guilty. Sebastian was so sweet and earnest standing there. And he looked at her with such desire that Chelsea couldn't help but hope that they would end up someplace secluded. Sebastian led her to a blanket far down on the sandy beach of the lakeshore. Although several other groups had the same idea and the beach was littered with blankets, it seemed more peaceful there, and Sebastian felt warm and solid as they sat side by side, their arms and legs touching. Chelsea grabbed a huge piece of the luscious cheesecake with her fork and fed it to Sebastian.

"Mmm . . . ," Sebastian murmured. "This is amazing. You know, this is my first Fourth of July in America."

"Well, you picked a really good one," Chelsea said. "The weather's perfect." Sebastian took the fork from her hand and began maneuvering a piece of cake toward her mouth. Chelsea leaned forward to catch it—she didn't want to risk another spill.

"Not just the weather," Sebastian said as the first firework whizzed high into the sky and burst into a shower of pyrotechnic white rain above their heads.

"Ooooooh," said the crowd. "Aaaaaaaah."

"Not just the weather?" Chelsea probed, picking a strawberry off the top of the cake and slipping it between Sebastian's lips. A little juice slipped out of the corner of his mouth, and she reached up to wipe it away with her finger.

"Yeah." Sebastian caught her hand, and with his other, he moved the plate of cheesecake away from them and onto the blanket. "It's everything: the fireworks, all of the people, the lake . . . you."

Chelsea was sure the rush of uncertainty she felt was just because she wasn't used to being romanced. Sebastian tried to feed her the last piece of cheesecake, but she held up her hand to stop him.

"I'm so full, I'm about to burst," she said apologetically.

Another firework exploded above their heads, and Sebastian looked at her. He smiled shyly, then moved his hand up and gently tilted Chelsea's chin. Their lips met softly, and Chelsea felt a short moment of panic. What if someone could see them: Sara, the other staffers, her parents or—even worse—Todd? She pulled back and looked around anxiously, but all the faces around them belonged to unfamiliar tourist families looking excitedly up at the fireworks show. Their faces dazzled in the darkness.

"Relax," Sebastian cooed, bringing Chelsea back to reality.

Chelsea smiled and touched the downy side of Sebastian's face, drawing him in toward her for a longer, more passionate kiss. She leaned in and gave herself up to Sebastian, letting the rest of the world fade away. Over their heads, the fireworks bloomed, burst, and faded, leaving gray trailers of smoke like fading flowers in the sky.

Chapter Eleven

Chelsea stood with her hands on her hips and stared at the colorful plastic bags laid out on her bed. She couldn't believe the sheer amount of shopping she had done that afternoon during her covert solo expedition to the mall in Reno. During her foray through Sara's closet several days before, she had tried on tons of clothes, noting sizes, colors, and labels, jotting each one down carefully in a small notebook—and armed with the notebook, she had taken the Meadowood Mall by storm.

Chelsea McCormick was going to arrive at the pool party that night dressed like a girl even if it killed her.

She reached into one of the many shopping bags littering the surface of her bed and pulled out a tiny brown bandeau-style bikini she still couldn't believe she had really just dropped eighty dollars on. She slipped off her clothes and carefully stepped into the new swimsuit, making sure it fit one last time before finally removing the tags.

For the first time in her life, Chelsea had forced herself to check out some fashion Web sites and magazines, which gave her a bunch of advice she found essentially useless. But they also told her a few important things, like that brown and teal were "in" this season. So, to complement her brown swimsuit, she had bought a simple turquoise necklace and a pair of matching earrings. She had also bought a short, sheer, cream-colored sarong to wrap around her hips. She was sure that wearing just the tiny bikini would make her feel like she was running around the party in her underwear.

Chelsea went to her computer and pulled up the Web page she'd bookmarked on "Effortless Sexy Hairdos." With a mouthful of bobby pins, she began the arduous process of creating a bun that looked like it had been haphazardly thrown together in a matter of seconds. *I can't believe I'm doing this,* she thought, wincing as she jammed another bobby pin into her head.

She had even bought herself a tube of mascara at Sephora. Waterproof, of course. After all, it *was* a pool party.

And then there were the shoes. Teenvogue.com had said that espadrilles were a great starting point for someone without a lot of experience wearing heels, plus they were totally cute for the summer. So Chelsea had found herself a pair that laced up the ankle. The woven rope heels were of a livable height, so she hoped she wouldn't go pitching forward into the pool.

Chelsea looked in the mirror, fully prepared to face a laughably grotesque impression of a gawky girl playing dress-up. But the woman who stared back at her was anything but gawky. Chelsea's new look was everything the fashion Web sites had promised . . . and more. The bikini looked great on her long, slim athletic body. The bandeau top made the most of her small chest, and the bottom scooped low to expose her firm stomach, with the sarong adding a touch of flirtiness and covering up her butt. Tendrils of hair curled out of her loose bun, softening her features, and the dangling turquoise earrings and touch of mascara drew attention to her eyes, which seemed larger and bluer than ever before. Her legs, which she normally considered her best feature anyway, seemed endless in the espadrilles, which gave her just enough lift to clearly define her muscular calves and thighs.

Chelsea had to admit to herself that she looked better than just "feminine" or "fashionable"—she looked *hot*!

Hopefully, everyone else would realize it, too. The skirt had worked for her at the barbecue the night before. Maybe now everyone would stop calling her nicknames that made her sound like a kid.

The clock on her nightstand read 12:27, and the party was supposed to have started at midnight—getting ready had taken longer than she had anticipated. Chelsea's stomach fluttered as she stepped quietly out of the house and down the dark path. As she approached the spa building, she was glad to see that the pool had steamed up the big glass windows. There was dim light emanating from within, but that was normal, since the safety lights around the pool stayed on all night. She was also pleased to note that if there was music playing, it wasn't loud enough for anyone outside to hear. So far, the staff were keeping their promises.

Chelsea glanced around quickly before opening the door, but the area around the spa was deserted. The only sound was the slight sighing of the pine trees in the wind. Most of the tourists had left that afternoon, piling into their SUVs with their faces red from too much sun and their children clutching fake souvenir arrowheads, already begging to come back. That left retirees and honeymooners for the most part: the former returning to their cabins early to sleep and the latter returning to their cabins early to not sleep.

Chelsea gasped as she entered the spa—it was almost as transformed as she was. Tiny votive candles burned all around the large kidney-shaped indoor pool, and a few even floated on its still surface. Aside from that, the only light in the building came from the pool's built-in

underwater lights, which gave the room a ghostly blue
glow and sent wavy shadows dancing across the ceiling.
Leo had set up a bar in the corner and was busy mixing
drinks behind it, and Death Cab for Cutie played softly
through the embedded speakers.

Even the summer staffers seemed artfully arranged,
standing in small groups on the mint-green tiles or
lounging, drinks in hand, on the chaises surrounding
the pool. Although small hand-printed signs reminded
everyone to be quiet, occasional exclamations and peals
of laughter burst loose and bounced around the room.
But as Chelsea closed the door and everyone looked up
to see who had joined them, the room went strangely
quiet. Everyone was looking at her in surprise: Nina,
Mel, and Sienna from the pool; Joel, Ted, and Leo over
by the bar; and Todd just emerging from the guys' locker
room. What was *he* doing there? How dare he show up
to the party he'd been bad-mouthing for days?

Suddenly feeling like an exotic zoo animal, Chelsea
waved. Several people waved back before returning to
their conversations, while Chelsea gratefully headed
across the room to get a drink. Her legs felt about a million miles long in the wedges, and she couldn't shake
the feeling that people were still scoping her out from
the corners of their eyes. What was really unnerving was
that she couldn't tell if they were checking her out in a
good way or not. Were all those staring eyes going,

"Wow, Chelsea looks hot," or, "Oh dear, what is Chelsea thinking?" She sneaked a glance back toward Todd and was surprised to see his eyes still glued to her, an unreadable expression on his face.

Chelsea approached the bar and noticed Sara leaning against it, staring at her through slitted eyes. Maybe she looked awful after all. . . .

"Nice swimsuit." Sara narrowed her eyes even further. "It kind of looks familiar. Where'd you get it?"

Chelsea's blush turned from rose to crimson. Without meaning to, she'd gotten a suit almost identical to one she'd secretly tried on from Sara's collection. Sara probably thought she'd borrowed it without asking. Not a far cry from the truth when Chelsea thought about the skirt from earlier. Chelsea had already put the skirt back where she'd found it, though there was still a tiny smudge of red near the hem that Chelsea hoped Sara wouldn't notice later. "I g-got it at Macy's in the Meadowood Mall in Reno. It's BCBG," Chelsea stammered. "Does it look okay?"

The moment Chelsea mentioned the designer, Sara's face relaxed into a smile. Chelsea was glad she'd remembered that Sara's own suit was Calvin Klein. And she was relieved that Sara wasn't wearing it that night, having opted instead for a flirty pale yellow string bikini that made her killer tan glow in contrast.

"It looks great on you." Sara's voice was warm and

sincere this time, and Chelsea felt a pang of guilt. She turned toward Leo, who was working the bar, and ordered a drink.

"You want the pool party special?" Leo winked as he poured a brilliant blue cocktail into a plastic cup and handed it to her. The beverage was cool in her hand as she eased away from the bar and went circling the pool in search of Sebastian.

"Hi, Chelsea," a voice behind her said. Chelsea froze in her tracks and turned to face Todd. Even as he flashed his trademark lopsided smile, his blue eyes looked icy. "I see Daddy's little girl got all dolled up for the big party."

"What?" Chelsea asked, annoyed. She suddenly felt extremely . . . exposed. "It's a pool party. I'm wearing a bathing suit. What's so weird about that?"

"You call *that* a bathing suit?" Todd asked. "I think those things are illegal in Utah."

Chelsea's cheeks blazed as her mind raced over the girls she had seen Todd with over the past few summers. Half of them had worn bikinis just as skimpy as hers out on the lake, so it wasn't like he had any right to judge.

"And pool parties are illegal at Glitterlake, too—as *you* have pointed out numerous times now," she spat back, putting one hand on her hip. "Yet here you are, Todd. What's up with that?"

Todd's Adam's apple bobbed in his throat as he

looked down at the floor, and Chelsea thought to herself that she totally had him there. *Next step: Toss him in the pool when he's not looking.*

"I, uh . . . wanted to see if Leo could pull it off," he mumbled.

"Ahem," Sebastian interrupted, joining them. Chelsea was positively mortified to see that he had opted to wear black Speedos instead of the baggy swim trunks or board shorts favored by every other guy on the resort staff. Granted, his slim, taut body looked unbelievably hot in them, but he was wearing less than she was. "You mean Leo and his faithful party consultant, Sebastian."

"Oh, you helped?" Todd tried to hide a smirk behind his cup, but Chelsea noticed it.

"The candles were my idea," Sebastian asserted. "What do you think?"

"They're beautiful," Chelsea assured him, taking his hand. "This place looks great."

"Thanks." Sebastian put his arm around her. "You look pretty good yourself. Want to hit the Jacuzzi?"

"Sure," Chelsea said, eager to get away from Todd's intense gaze.

Sebastian waved good-bye, and the two of them headed toward the hot tub.

"I can't believe you're wearing a Speedo," Chelsea whispered, giggling as she untied her espadrilles and eased her way into the foamy water, leaving her sarong in a pile with the shoes.

"Why?" Sebastian seemed genuinely puzzled. "This is what we wear at home."

"But nobody wears them here," Chelsea pointed out.

"So?" Sebastian shrugged. "This is what I'm used to, and I'd rather be comfortable than wear something I don't like, just to fit in."

Sebastian's words hit dangerously close to home as Chelsea looked down at the wavy lines of her bikini through the hot tub's frothy surface. Was that what she was doing? She didn't exactly feel comfortable, but having people tell her she looked hot was a refreshing change.

Just then Todd appeared above them on the Jacuzzi's edge, a cold can of beer in his hand.

"Hey." He stepped into the water. "Mind if I join you guys? The hot tub seemed like a good idea."

Chelsea's heartbeat sped up as Todd slipped onto the bench next to her. What was he doing? Did he know something was going on with her and Sebastian? The strong drink in her hand was starting to make her head spin. She slid it away, thinking she had probably had enough, especially given the way her body temperature was suddenly rising. She couldn't tell if it was from the Jacuzzi's heat or from being between Sebastian and Todd in such a small place—and while wearing so little clothing. She'd never felt so exposed . . . and the strange thing was that some part of her liked it. In a weird, nerve-racking way.

"So how's it going, Sebastian?" Todd leaned slightly over Chelsea to direct his question. "How are you adjusting to American life?"

"It's nice," Sebastian said, sounding strangely guarded. "So far, everyone I've met has been really friendly."

"Yeah, has Chelsea been showing you around a lot?" Todd persisted. "I mean, she's the best person to get to know here at Glitterlake, since she's the owners' kid. You knew that, right? Mark McCormick, Patty McCormick, and Little McCormick here." He put an arm around Chelsea's shoulders, spiking her body temperature even more. *What* was going on?

"The whole McCormick family has been very sweet to me," Sebastian replied neutrally. His hand found Chelsea's under the water, and he squeezed it tightly. "And I've been very lucky to have Chelsea around."

Todd removed his arm from around Chelsea's shoulders to reach for his beer, and Chelsea let out her breath slowly. She hadn't even realized she'd been holding it.

Sebastian seemed finished with Todd. He turned away from him and leaned in toward Chelsea. "Hey, Chels, c'mere," he smirked, glancing at Todd out of the corner of his eyes. "I want to tell you something."

"What?" Chelsea caught Todd rolling his eyes as he sipped his beer. She felt really weirded out by the dynamic between the guys. It was almost like Sebastian could read her mind about Todd—and didn't much like what he saw.

"This." Sebastian leaned forward and kissed her gently on the lips, taking another sly look in Todd's direction. Chelsea's eyes flew open just wide enough to catch the shock that registered on Todd's face. Chelsea panicked for a minute and then just became annoyed. Why did Sebastian have to kiss her in public like that? It was just so, so . . .

So like she and Sebastian were actually, *officially* dating, she realized as Sebastian's strong arms wrapped around her back. And if Sebastian was her boyfriend for real, then who cared if Todd saw her kissing him? It wasn't like he never kissed those flirty tourist girls—it was perfectly fair for Chelsea to get a little action, too. She closed her eyes and melted into Sebastian's kiss. Gently, she opened her mouth a little and let her tongue touch Sebastian's. He moved in closer, breathing a little heavier as he held Chelsea around her bare waist.

Suddenly Sebastian stiffened in her arms and quickly tried to pull away. A white-hot light flashed behind her eyes, and Chelsea opened them quickly. All the lights in the building were on, the music had stopped, and dead silence rang out over the tiled spa. She pulled away from Sebastian and saw the very last thing she wanted to see right then: her father.

Chapter Twelve

W hat. Is. Going. On. Here." Anger blazed in Mark McCormick's eyes as he spoke slowly and evenly. Chelsea gulped hard. She felt the eyes of the entire room on her—and not in the admiring-from-afar way they'd all been checking her out earlier. She could tell that as much as they wanted to be somewhere else at that moment, her fellow summer staffers were equally glad that they weren't her.

She would have liked not to be herself right then, too. She couldn't believe she had disappointed her dad: the one person in her life she had always tried to make proud. What exactly was it that had made her think the pool party was a good idea?

Chelsea knew she had to say something: This was all

her fault, and she had to own up to it. She was about to speak when a voice other than hers burst in and answered her father. Sebastian hurried to join her. "It's not what it looks like, Mr. McCormick," he said. "A few of us just happened to be walking by and—"

Chelsea winced and grasped Sebastian's arm, hoping to quiet him. She knew that as much as her father hated people breaking his rules, he hated being lied to even more.

"I don't want to hear another word from you!" Mark McCormick roared. "Not after watching you molest my daughter in the hot tub. I'm half inclined to send you packing back to Brazil right now, no questions asked."

Anger burned the back of Chelsea's throat. As angry as she was at herself, she couldn't believe that her dad would say something so rude to Sebastian in front of the entire staff. Suddenly she stepped forward.

"Sebastian was *not* molesting me," she said through the fire in her mouth. She could feel her cheeks positively glowing with rage and embarrassment, but she couldn't stop. She'd gotten everyone into this mess, and there was no reason for Sebastian to take the blame. "We were kissing—that's all."

Her dad's eyes narrowed as she continued, and she realized that one of the few good things about never having had a boyfriend was never having had to deal with the awkwardness of bringing one home to her strong-willed, protective father.

"Just kissing," Chelsea repeated quietly. A note of pleading crept into her voice. "Dad, I'm sixteen. It's normal."

"Normal?" her father asked incredulously. "To be doing it in a Jacuzzi? Past midnight? And wearing *that*?"

The entire staff gasped, and Chelsea felt her knees go weak. She had never felt more miserable, embarrassed, or just plain exposed in her life.

"And what about the rest of you?" Mark asked fiercely, glancing around the room at the guilty revelers. "As staff, I'm sure you're all aware that the spa building closes at nine p.m. on Sundays. It seems to me that being here after normal hours would be a *really big mistake*."

Chelsea gulped hard. *Oh yeah*. There was that, too. She wanted to be anywhere else in the world right then, but she forced herself to look her dad in the eye. "I'm sorry," she said. "We wanted to have a party here, so I took the keys. I knew it was wrong and I did it anyway. We had a plan to clean up and everything, but that doesn't make it right. If you want to ground me, I understand."

Her dad shook his head slowly. "No. Cleaning it up doesn't make it right," he said. "Chelsea, I'm disappointed in you. You know how devastating it would be for me and your mother if something happened to this building or any of you *in* it—and at the height of tourist season, too."

"I know," Chelsea said quietly. Now her father had switched from anger to disappointment, and that made it even worse. She couldn't bear to look in his eyes.

"Excuse me, Mr. McCormick." Chelsea's stomach turned when Todd stepped forward. "This wasn't all Chelsea's fault. It's true that she took the keys, but . . . well, some of us kind of talked her into doing it. I feel bad saying that, Mr. McCormick, but it's true. So if Chelsea gets in trouble, we should all get in trouble. At least, people like me who have been here for a while and know the score."

The very last thing Chelsea expected was for Todd to come out and defend her. And at risk not only to himself, but also to the rest of the staff—when he himself had warned them not to do it. But all around the room she heard people murmuring their assent.

"It's true," Leo said, stepping away from the bar and toward Mark McCormick. "I did most of the organizing and setting up."

"I helped, too," Sara confessed. Chelsea was shocked that her perfect half sister would admit to such a breach of trust.

"And having a pool party was my idea to begin with," Sebastian added.

"Well." Mark McCormick's eyes still flashed as he looked around the room, but Chelsea could tell from the way his jaw loosened under his beard that he wasn't as angry as he'd been just a few moments before. "I'm not thrilled about you kids choosing to have a party here. You could have done a lot of damage and put Glitterlake at a huge risk both with safety and finances. I intend for your actions to have consequences."

Chelsea held her breath as her dad paused either for dramatic effect or to figure out how he was going to go about punishing the entire staff. He had always been pretty tough on her when she broke the rules. The winter she was five, he had caught her crayoning on the wall of her bedroom, and not only had he taken away her crayons for a *whole year*, but he'd also made her help them repaint the walls, which had been fun for about ten minutes until her little arms got tired. This time it was far worse, though. She'd betrayed his trust. And it felt terrible—with or without punishment.

Her dad stroked his beard. The whole staff seemed to be holding its breath. "Now that we've got these plant walks going, I've been meaning to get around to repairing the Breakneck Ridge Trail," her dad murmured as if thinking out loud. Chelsea, Leo, and a few of the other longtime staffers groaned softly. The Breakneck Ridge Trail snaked up the side of Eagle Mountain, a steep series of switchbacks gaining over a thousand feet in elevation before running along the ridge for two and a half miles and descending down the other side. The trail had fallen into disrepair over the last few years from heavy erosion, and the McCormicks hadn't bothered to fix it, choosing instead to focus on the easier trails, family recreation, and the water sports program. The last time Chelsea had been up there, the trail had been a mess, rocky and uneven, with several trees fallen across it. Repairing it would be a nightmare.

"Yup." Her dad reached into the back pocket of his well-worn Wranglers for the small notebook he always carried around. "I'm going to take down the names of everyone here—and you are going to have that trail tourist-ready by the weekend rush on Friday. It's a lot of work, but I'm sure that if all of you are willing to put this much work into a party, you'll be more than happy to give your all to a trail that *everyone* can enjoy. Right?"

Everyone tried to sound like they hadn't just been assigned to five days of hard labor in the hot, high-altitude sun as they murmured their agreement.

"Good." Mark McCormick seemed pretty proud of his idea. He had the beginnings of a smile on his lips and the flashes of anger in his eyes had almost turned to twinkles. "Now, let me start taking down names."

Chapter Thirteen

In Chelsea's dream, she was jumping on a trampoline in the middle of the lake. Each time she jumped, she went higher and higher in the air, and with every jump she was able to do more complex inverts and rolls. She looked out over the lake and saw another boat about a hundred feet away. The boat also had a trampoline on it, and Todd was jumping up and down on that trampoline. Every time Chelsea came down, he sprang up. She could tell he was trying to outdo her and she didn't want to let him, so she decided to try the hardest move in wakeboarding history. As she got ready to spring into the air, Todd yelled to her and pointed down at the water below them. He said something, but she couldn't hear.

"What?" she called out to him.

Todd's voice sounded very far away and very panicked. "Sharks!" he cried.

Chelsea had already jumped into the air, but when she turned upside down on the first invert, she could see the fins circling beneath her. She overcompensated and was falling toward shark-infested waters!

"Chelsea, Chelsea, Chelsea . . . ," Todd called after her as she was about to smack down onto the surface.

"Chelsea!" Chelsea awoke with a start, the blankets twisted in a mess around her sweaty body. Someone was knocking on the door to her room, calling her name. Outside her window, the sky was still the steel-gray color of dawn. "Chelsea, time to get up."

Chelsea sat up and rubbed her head, which ached and felt full of fuzz, probably from the cup of "pool punch" the night before. "Mom, it's July," she protested. "I don't need to be up for school until September."

"Your dad wanted all of you to get an early start on the Ridge," her mom explained. "He's at the barracks waking up the rest of the staff right now. Don't forget to wear your work boots!"

She has got to be kidding. Chelsea dragged herself out of bed. But she knew her mom wasn't kidding. She grabbed an old pair of jeans and her cruddiest Tahoe Half-Pipe Cruisers T-shirt and pulled them on, padding to the bathroom to brush her teeth. She knew there was no point in showering—she would just smell like a horse's rear end by noon. And probably feel like one, too. Well, even more than she already did.

Downstairs, even Sara looked like she was dragging. She wordlessly slid a box of Honey Nut Crunch across the table to Chelsea, who dumped it in a bowl, poured milk over it, and began crunching.

"Well, girls!" Their dad came into the kitchen looking as refreshed and jubilant as if he hadn't been up half the night busting his teenage daughter's illicit pool party. "Ready to work?"

"Sure," Sara said, trying for her usual bright tone and falling slightly flat.

"Do we have a choice?" Chelsea grumbled.

"You did," her dad said diplomatically, "when you decided to take the keys to the spa and throw that little soiree of yours. That's when you made your choice."

"Dad," Chelsea said, willing herself not to cry. She got up and rinsed her bowl, then walked over to her father and looked him in the eye. "I really am sorry."

Mark McCormick chuckled a bit. "Not as sorry as you will be. Hey, Chelsea, can I talk to you for a second?" her father asked, walking out to the porch.

Chelsea followed him, nervous about what he could have to say. She stood at the railing, looking over the misty lake reflecting the bright early-morning sunlight. "What's up?" she asked.

"Chelsea, you know I'm disappointed in you," her dad began, putting his hands in his pockets. He turned to face her.

"Dad, I know I–," she began. She felt horrible for letting her dad down and couldn't remember the last time she'd seen him looking so angry and hurt.

"No, let me finish," he said sternly. "Chelsea, your mother and I have been talking and I . . . we . . . we don't think that you should see Sebastian anymore. I know you'll be in contact with him here at the resort, but we would prefer it if you didn't date him."

"What!" Chelsea was shocked. Of all the things that her dad could have said–that she couldn't compete, that he didn't want her to teach, that she was grounded, even!–she never expected him to say this. She put her hands on the railing and watched her knuckles turn white. "Dad, this has nothing to do with Sebastian!" she said, hearing her voice rise.

"Chelsea, there is no negotiating here. This is not a discussion. We just don't think he's a good influence. Really, Champ, this is for the best," he said, looking at Chelsea and putting his hand on her shoulder. "Now get ready to go."

Chelsea refused to look at her father and stared out over the water for a few more minutes, seething. *How dare they!* Chelsea stormed back inside, slamming the door. Now she was actually looking forward to getting out on the trail. At least it would let her work out some of her anger.

* * *

"Wow, Dad can be a real slave driver," Sara said as they trudged toward the Breakneck Ridge trailhead. Chelsea's stomach dropped. It was really disconcerting to hear someone else refer to *her* father as "Dad."

"I guess he just wants there to be consequences for doing the wrong thing." Even though she was really angry with him, she still felt like she had to defend him.

"No, it's good," Sara said quickly. "I mean, he's really fair. Not like . . . Well, some parents will punish you for all the wrong things but then also kind of let you get away with murder."

Chelsea didn't want Sara to praise her dad. Chelsea already knew he was fair. He always did the right thing. He had always been the best dad, and she had always been the best daughter she could. Until now. She looked miserably at her hiking shoes.

"Hey," Sara said as they neared the trailhead, interrupting Chelsea's thoughts. She slowed down her pace a little, so that Chelsea had no choice but to slow down to match her. "I wanted to tell you—it was really cool the way you stood up to Dad last night." Sara's words came out in a rush. It was the first time Chelsea had ever seen her embarrassed.

"You mean when I told him that I took the keys?" she asked. Just remembering the moment made her cringe.

"Well, that, yeah," Sara said. "But I mean, not *just* that. All of it. Like when you said it's normal to kiss boys, and when you offered to take the blame for everything and just . . . the way you wouldn't let Sebastian lie to save your butt. It was really cool."

"Thanks," Chelsea said slowly. She was touched by Sara's praise and didn't know what else to say.

"Sure." And then they were at the trailhead with all the rest of the summer staff, who rubbed their eyes and complained softly as they sorted through piles of gear.

"Let's hear it for the guests of honor!" Leo called with faux-cheery sarcasm as they approached, and the rest of the staff burst out in half-ironic applause. "As the moron who threw the party together and provided the refreshments, I've also been tasked with heading up the trail crew. Chelsea, I put together a pack especially for you." He bent down and picked up an enormous canvas sack bursting with the heavy steel rebar pieces that were used to prevent erosion up on the trails. "We'll be starting at the top of the ridge and working our way back down. Enjoy."

"Ouch, Leo . . . rebar?" she asked. "Up all those switchbacks?"

"Here, take this, too," Leo said, handing her a heavy iron pickax. "You can strap it to the side of the pack."

"You have *got* to be kidding me," Chelsea groaned.

"Um . . . are you the one who stole the keys?" Leo asked. "Was it *your* dad who caught *you* in a red-hot lip-lock in the Jacuzzi?" Chelsea's face turned scarlet. Leo grinned and punched her lightly on the arm. "Chill out, sport," he laughed, and leaned closer to her. "That's not why you're carrying the rebar. You're doing it because you're the toughest mofo at Glitterlake and you won't start complaining halfway up. Oh, one more thing—you'll be working with Todd. Have fun!"

*　　*　　*

By the end of the day, Chelsea's shoulders ached from swinging the pick and pounding rebar into the trail. In between bouts of attacking the rocky soil with all the strength her upper body could muster, Chelsea gulped water and stared at the way Todd's muscles flexed each time he heaved the heavy tool into the earth.

Everyone was in a pretty grouchy mood, but her day brightened a little when her mom showed up around lunchtime with peanut-butter-and-jelly sandwiches and lemonade made from scratch. Then things got even better when Todd stripped off his sweat-soaked T-shirt and handed Chelsea a bottle of Bug n' Sun SPF 15, casually asking if she would do his back.

Chelsea tried not to linger too long on each of the depressions between his perfect muscles, but his skin under her hands was way more pleasant than anything she had ever felt—including making out with Sebastian. She stroked sunscreen into the taut, tan sides of his lower back. She was sure by the time she finally dragged her hands away that Todd was going to turn her around and accuse her of sexually harassing him. But instead he just muttered something that sounded like "Don't stop."

"What?" Chelsea wondered if she had misheard.

"Nothing." Todd turned around and gave her a lop-sided grin. "Hey, you may want to put some on your nose—it's starting to look red."

Chelsea squeezed a big white blob of sunscreen onto her finger and started smearing it onto her nose. When she looked up at Todd, he was chuckling.

"What's so funny this time?" she asked, feeling irritated. She hated being laughed at—and she was still feeling especially sensitive after last night.

"You look like Bozo the Clown," Todd sputtered. He reached out and tweaked her nose with his finger, then turned it around to show her all the sunblock that hadn't rubbed in.

"Hey, how come you two aren't working?" a voice

boomed from down the trail. Mark McCormick lumbered into view, his face red and sweaty from the climb in the mid-afternoon sun.

"We were just taking a water break, sir," Todd explained.

"You two didn't sign on to be slackers when you decided to throw that little shindig last night, did you?" His words sounded firm, but Chelsea's dad was smiling.

Chelsea and Todd shook their heads.

"Well, I don't want to see you start now. Grab your picks and get to work!" Mark stood over them as they sheepishly picked up their tools and started chipping at the hard soil alongside the trail. By the time Chelsea turned around, her father was gone . . . and Todd had stopped working again and was leaning on his pick, staring at her.

"What?" she asked, suddenly feeling as exposed in her work boots and T-shirt as she had in her bikini the night before.

"So . . . what's up with you and Sebastian?" Todd asked.

"What do you mean, what's up?" Chelsea couldn't believe she was finally getting to turn the tables on Todd. Todd, who always dated the prettiest tourists at Glitterlake while she had nobody and had to settle for only getting to hang out with him out on the water.

"Well . . . ," Todd shifted from foot to foot. Even his

uncomfortable shifting was graceful. "I mean, I was with you guys in the Jacuzzi last night. Have you been, like, together for a while?"

"Nothing's going on, really . . . ," she said mysteriously. If the thought of Chelsea dating Sebastian got under Todd's skin the way it looked like it did, Chelsea was not going to let a little thing like getting in trouble keep her from pursuing him. Sebastian, that is.

Todd gave her a funny, crooked little smile. "You're acting weird."

Chelsea wanted to tell him that if she was acting weird, it was only because she'd spent so many years longing for him that it had stunted her emotional development as far as relationships were concerned. Now she was making up for lost time with Sebastian—who just happened to be gorgeous. And to have a hot accent. But of course, there was no way she could tell Todd that. Fortunately, Leo interrupted the moment by barreling up to them, clapping his hands and whistling.

"Time's *up!*" he called. "Go home, wash off the grime, and I don't want to see you until tomorrow." Without waiting for a reply, he took off toward the next group of workers farther up the trail.

Todd and Chelsea looked at each other and cracked up.

"So," Chelsea said as her giggles subsided, "want to hit the lake?"

"Well . . . ," Todd replied, leaning on his pick, still

smiling his cute half smile. "I've been doing heavy manual labor all day, I'm exhausted, every muscle in my body
aches, and now you want to go exercise some more?"

"But it's not work," Chelsea pleaded. "It's play!"

Todd's smile widened, and he leaned in closer to her.
Her head swam as she breathed in his sexy scent of sunscreen and sweat, and for one dizzying moment she
thought he was going to kiss her. Instead, he moved to
the side and whispered in her ear. "I like the way you
think," he said as he turned and started running down
the mountain. "Last one to the dock has to drive first!"

*　　*　　*

As Chelsea watched Todd in the rearview mirror, she
couldn't help being amazed at the way he moved gracefully in and out of the wake. She had spent hours and
hours of her life watching the pros and semi-pros board
in person, on DVD, and on YouTube, and Todd was *not*
the best. He wasn't the strongest, the lightest, or the
fastest, and he certainly didn't jump the highest or do
the splashiest grabs.

But Chelsea had always thought that Todd was the
most capable of making wakeboarding a beautiful sport.
His body moved with grace and precision; he had a perfect economy of movement and always seemed to know
exactly where he was going and what he was doing. Even

if he ended up on his butt, his body just *flowed*. He soared through the air, hovering over the water before coming back down in a perfect white spray of foam. Every move was precise, deliberate, and incalculably beautiful, and watching him made Chelsea's chest tighten with both admiration and longing. It was like she was falling in love with him all over again.

Which she just couldn't allow herself to do. It would hurt too much. It already did.

"Good ride," Chelsea complimented him when he returned to the boat and stripped his wetsuit down to his waist.

"Thanks." Todd leaned over her to get a towel, and his hair fell forward, dripping water onto her arm.

"Sorry," he murmured, smiling almost shyly as he offered her the towel to dry off.

"It's cool." Chelsea could barely meet his eyes. "I'll be soaked in a minute anyway."

"True," Todd acknowledged. "Hey, did you see that triple handle pass I pulled earlier? How'd it look?"

"All right," Chelsea said, smiling.

Todd playfully rolled the towel into a rattail and swatted it at her butt. "All right, yourself," he grumbled. "You get out there and try to top me!"

Plunging into the cool, clean lake water after a long day in the sun was almost more refreshing than her easy banter with Todd. *Maybe he really does like me after all,*

Chelsea thought as she swam out into the wake and found her footing atop the board. *Maybe we can be more than just competitors . . . maybe we can even be more than just friends.* But wait . . . what was she thinking? She already *had* a boyfriend, and Sebastian was great. He was certainly nicer to her than Todd had ever been—even when she and Todd were getting along, it was more because those were the times she could tolerate his rough teasing. He treated her more like a kid sister than like a potential girlfriend, so why did her hormones always go into overdrive when he was around? Chelsea shook her head and wished she could eliminate boys from her mind. This was her precious time out on the water, and she intended to make the most of it.

Instead of launching straight into her usual gonzo tricks, Chelsea tried to emulate Todd's smooth, reserved movements, concentrating on the way her body flowed with the water. She picked up momentum and tried a backside 360 spin, Todd style. She landed perfectly and gave a thumbs-up to Todd. After a few more tricks, though, she gave up trying to board like Todd and rode full-out Chelsea style, pulling out the big guns and trying all her favorite tricks.

Seeing that she was on a roll, Todd maneuvered the boat in a big circle, obviously trying to challenge her. But Chelsea was always up for a challenge. She eased away from the wake as Todd brought the boat back through it, giving her a double-up that would create a wake twice the size. That meant more air if she timed it right. As the boat passed through the wake she started to edge in, her stomach already clenching deliciously at the thought of the kick-ass whirlybird 540 she was about to throw down. She'd put Todd's arrogance to shame forever with this next move.

She hit the wake hard with the nose of her board and flew into the air, higher than she was used to, twisting her body into an invert as the wind rushed past her ears and the blue sparkles of water nearly blinded her. She was upside down in the air when she looked down and realized she had timed the jump wrong: She was still high enough in the air that if she didn't flip over one more time, she was going to have a lot of dead time to get off balance and probably fall on her butt—unless she added another turn.

She had never gone for a whirlybird 720 before. In fact, very few wakeboarders had *ever* actually landed one. But she had adrenaline and talent on her side—well, that and an overwhelming desire to show Todd how good she could be when she was at the top of her game.

Just as she went into the final leg of her invert, though, she looked down and realized that the water was rushing toward her much faster than she had thought. Had she miscalculated just how high she was in the air? She flailed her arms, hoping to break her fall, and the toeside edge of her board caught the water.

For a moment, the entire world seemed to stop moving. And then Chelsea pitched forward into what may very well have been the *absolute worst* face-plant in all of wakeboarding history.

Chapter Fourteen

Everything was blurry when she surfaced a moment later. She shook her head, and the blue and green smudges finally separated out into a lake, trees, and mountains. Someone was yelling her name.

"Chelsea!" Todd still looked a little hazy as he cut the motor, dropped anchor, and leapt off the side, his face a mess of worry and concern. Before she knew it, he was at her side in the water. He slid his hand under her armpits and dragged her back to the boat.

"I still know how to swim!" Chelsea tried to wriggle free from his grasp. But suddenly she wasn't so sure. Her arm hurt where it had hit her bindings. Like, *really* hurt. Like, hurt so much that if she thought about it too long, she might start to cry. And there was no *way* she was going to start crying in front of Todd.

He didn't say anything, just dragged her over the side of the boat, deposited her in the passenger's seat, and frantically began pulling up the anchor.

"How many fingers am I holding up?" He quickly turned back to Chelsea.

"Four," Chelsea said. "Todd, you're being ridiculous. I'm fine." But her voice shook as she said it, and her arm pulsed with pain.

"I'm getting you back to shore and to the hospital *now*," Todd insisted. He started the boat and began speeding across the water, continually looking back at Chelsea every few seconds. For a while there was only the sound of the boat's motor and the wind. Chelsea looked at Todd and noticed that his jaw was set in a sharp, angry line. "What's wrong?" she asked.

"What's *wrong*?" Todd exploded. "You were acting like an idiot out there! What the *hell* were you thinking, trying for a seven-twenty? Half the pros can't even get that move!"

The bolt of adrenaline that shot through her was almost enough to eclipse the pain in her arm. "Are you trying to say I'm not good enough?" she snapped back in defense. "I've never seen *you* try anything more challenging than a three-sixty, so don't even go there."

"That's because I'm not stupid!" Todd screamed

back. Chelsea had never seen him so angry. "I know my limits, and I don't go trying tricks that are way out of my league."

"I'm not stupid! And if you didn't want me to try something new, why the hell did you give me a double-up?" Chelsea asked.

"I wouldn't have if I'd known you were going to do that," Todd said through clenched teeth. "I wanted you to have fun—I didn't want you to break your neck." Todd looked like he was disgusted with her. "I can't believe your dad is even letting you teach, if you're going to go pulling dumb-ass stunts like that."

"Teaching has *nothing* to do with it!" Chelsea yelled back at him. Tears stung the corners of her eyes, but she willed herself to keep them at bay. She tried to speak calmly. "I may not have landed that trick, but that doesn't mean I can't. You're just jealous because you *never* will."

Todd's knuckles turned white on the wheel, and the muscles in his jaw twitched. He wouldn't even look at her now. He opened his mouth to scold her back, but nothing came out.

Chelsea gritted her teeth against the pain in her arm and looked out over the water. The pain was getting so bad now, she could barely keep her eyes open. She clenched them shut, leaning against the side of the boat.

*　　*　　*

Chelsea awoke in the hospital. She vaguely remembered Todd carrying her off the boat. But he was gone now.

"See that?" A doctor who had just entered her room slapped an X-ray of Chelsea's arm onto the light-box. "Fractured in three places. You're going to need a pretty big cast for that to heal." He was a roly-poly, jovial Santa Claus type in tiny wire-rimmed glasses, and his chuckle made Chelsea's skin crawl. Her arm was killing her, but the last thing she wanted was a cast the size of a small European country. It would totally throw off her balance while she was on the board.

"Can you please at least cut out the fingers so I can still hold the towrope?" she asked.

The doctor's laugh came from deep in his sizable belly. "I don't reckon it matters that much, sweet pea," he said. *Sweet pea?* "You're going to have keep that thing well away from the water for the next six to eight weeks."

"Six to eight *weeks!*" Chelsea's entire summer flashed before her eyes. "But I can't wait that long. There's the Challenge! I still have a ton of practicing to do. Plus what about teaching? I have to teach—it's my *job!*"

"But your health comes first." The doctor gave her a kind smile. Chelsea wanted to strangle him.

"Now you just sit here with your mother," he said, speaking to her as if she were five years old, "and a nurse will be in soon to get you prepped and put on the cast."

"There's no way you can keep me off the water!" Chelsea looked around in a huff to see her mother standing in the doorway, giving her a distressed look. "What?" she asked.

"Could you please try to be more polite?" Patty asked.

"But he's trying to tell me I can't compete in the Challenge!" Chelsea protested. "There's no way that's happening–there is just *no way*."

Patty's distressed look deepened, and her brows creased. "I wish you weren't so stubborn," she sighed. "Because with your safety and health involved, you can't ride until that cast is off."

"What? I can't believe you!" Chelsea exploded. "Oh, right, if you had it your way, I'd spend all my time putting on pretty dresses and chasing after plants like Sara." She hardly knew where all this anger was coming from— it just kept bubbling out.

"Honey, I know you're upset, but you don't have to take it out on your sister," her mom said.

"Half sister," Chelsea snapped automatically.

"I wish you'd stop saying that," Patty said. "It's hurtful, you know. She's your family, too," Patty continued. "Even though you don't know her that well and are living with her for the first time, you should treat her like a sister."

"Oh, you mean the way you treat her like a daughter?" Chelsea asked, thinking of all the times her mom had gone with Sara to the designer outlet mall and the two of them had returned gossiping and hauling shopping bags. Her mom *never* did stuff like that with her. Never mind that Chelsea hated shopping.

"I'm just trying to make her feel at home," Patty said through compressed lips. She was clearly surprised by what Chelsea had said. "Sara hasn't had the easiest time of it, you know."

Chelsea was about to ask what was so awful about Sara's seemingly perfect life when the nurse bustled in, pushing a squeaking silver cart piled high with blades, bandages, and sterilizing sprays. She shaved Chelsea's arm and began to wrap it in plaster, and Chelsea watched her mother out of the corner of her eye. Whatever it was that her mom thought was so great about Sara, Chelsea knew that *she* didn't have it.

Her mom leaned over and kissed Chelsea on the forehead. "Does it hurt, honey?" she asked.

Chelsea nodded and bit her lip. It hurt a lot. Not just her arm, but her whole life.

Chapter Fifteen

Chelsea's mom maneuvered her Camry up the resort's long, curved gravel driveway and Chelsea could hear music and voices coming from the deck outside the main lodge overlooking the lake. As they drew closer, she could see her father strumming a guitar, and Sara and Leo sitting next to him.

Instead of pulling the car around to the small private driveway by their house, her mom drove into an empty parking space in the public lot around the lodge and got out, motioning for Chelsea to follow her.

Chelsea sighed as she got out of the car. She wasn't really in the mood to socialize, and the cast on her arm seemed to weigh about a thousand extra pounds. She felt like it was dragging her to the side so that she lumbered like an ape instead of walking upright.

Her mom pushed open the sliding glass doors to the deck, and Chelsea stepped through. Suddenly everyone stopped talking and burst into applause.

Chelsea looked around, disoriented and confused.

"Welcome home!" everyone yelled. "Get well soon!"

Chelsea glanced from the crowd to her cast and back again. She had been gone for only a few hours, but people were acting as if she had just returned from a decade-long foray into the third world. Before she could even ask what was going on, she had been hustled into a chair, and a plate with a burger, potato salad, and corn materialized in front of her. Someone else handed her a tall glass of lemonade, and then Sienna came over and thrust a greeting card in her hands. It had a picture of a sad-looking dog with a hot water bottle on its head and said, "Don't be a sick puppy—get well soon!" When she opened it, the inside was a mess of signatures and get-well wishes in different-colored ink.

"But all I did was break my arm," she said dazedly, looking up at the sea of faces.

"Well, your mom called your dad from the hospital and told him how upset you were that you wouldn't be able to compete in the Challenge," Sienna explained. "And a bunch of us were there and we felt really bad for you, so we figured we'd have a little party to try and cheer you up."

Chelsea felt her face go hot. Panic was rising in her throat.

"Who says I'm not competing in the Challenge?"

"Me," a deep voice above her head said. She turned around to see her father staring down at her with his hands on his hips and a don't-mess-with-me look in his eyes. "The doctor told you to stay off the water and he meant it. Your mother and I mean it, too. From now on, no practicing until you're better. You can still teach, but you need to stay in the boat. That's as close to the water as you're going to get."

"But . . ." Chelsea realized she was about to start whining in front of everyone and stopped. She figured that going against her dad was maybe not the best idea she'd ever had, considering she was still in trouble for the pool party. It seemed like she couldn't do anything right anymore. She stared down at her blue Puma running shoes.

"There will be other chances, honey," her mom said, appearing at her side and rubbing her back.

Then Sara emerged through the sliding glass doors, struggling under the weight of two trays of freshly baked, newly frosted, pastel-colored cupcakes. She even looked a bit like a cupcake herself, in a lemon-yellow sundress and low white peep-toe pumps. The crowd that had been gathered around Chelsea a moment ago now turned and buzzed toward Sara, reaching for cupcakes even before she had set them down on the table. Everyone exclaimed over the cupcakes: how perfect they looked, how delicious they tasted, how moist and fresh they were. Sara had even decorated them with botanically correct Tahoe region wildflowers done in frosting.

"I had no idea Sara could bake!" Chelsea's mom said to her dad as they stood by the railing, his arm around her as they each munched a cupcake and looked out over the lake.

"Sara has a lot of talents," her dad said proudly. "I just wish Olivia had done more to encourage them. It seems like all she's ever cared about is Sara landing a rich boyfriend."

They were talking quietly, and Chelsea could tell they didn't intend for her to hear. They probably thought she was hovering over by the food table with everyone else instead of still sitting shell-shocked in the same chair she'd been herded into when she arrived.

"Well, we can try *our* best." Patty rested her head on Mark's shoulder. "It's been so nice having her here this summer."

"I agree," Chelsea's dad said. "Maybe we can have her back next summer, too."

"I'd like that, Mark," Patty said, lovingly nestling closer to her husband.

Chelsea's head drooped. Sara was the good, sweet daughter who stayed out of everyone's way and always did the right thing, and she, Chelsea, was the bad daughter who threw illegal pool parties and got in accidents doing daredevil stunts. She watched Sara throw back her head and laugh at something Leo had said, her legs and neck and chest a series of perfect smooth lines, her hair and dress complementary shades of the same color. Most of the rest of the summer staffers gathered around Leo, who was telling another of his famous stories. Chelsea knew she should join them, but she felt too sad. She felt like something was missing. And then she realized what it was: Todd wasn't there at the party. He was probably still angry about what she had said on the way back to shore. And she didn't blame him, either. Things had actually been going well between them for once. Just thinking about it made the back of her throat feel scratchy and hot. Why did she have to go and mess it all up?

She wondered where he was. *Probably off with Vanessa or some other tourist chick,* she thought miserably.

"Hi, sweetie." Sebastian approached her and held out a plate with a pink-frosted cupcake decorated with a daisy. "I brought you one, since you're injured."

"Uhm, okay . . . ," Chelsea said, taking the plate as Sebastian pulled a chair close to hers and sat down. She looked nervously toward her parents, but luckily, they weren't looking in her direction. "My arm's broken, not my leg."

"Sorry," Sebastian muttered, looking hurt. She felt bad. It was like her own personal say-the-wrong-thing day.

"No, I'm sorry. It's not you. I'm just depressed. But thanks for the cupcake," she amended, taking a bite. It actually *was* pretty good.

"How's your arm?" Sebastian asked, his big dark eyes full of concern.

"Hurts," Chelsea admitted. "And this cast is huge. I hate it."

"I'm sorry. I was so worried about you when I found out. I know how much wakeboarding means to you. And competing in the Challenge."

"Yeah, it sucks," Chelsea said. Just thinking about it made the world feel huge and empty. "A lot."

"Well, maybe this will help." Sebastian grinned mischievously as he pulled a red Sharpie marker from the pocket of his plaid Bermuda shorts. He reached out and took hold of her cast, gently trailing his fingers down the part of her arm that was still exposed in a way that made her shiver and look around nervously to see if anyone had noticed. By the time she ascertained that the other partygoers were too involved in their own conversations to notice anything going on with her and Sebastian, Chelsea looked down at her cast to see that he had scrawled his name with a winking face underneath.

Chelsea forced herself to smile as she realized she would now have to think about Sebastian every time she looked at her arm. But what was wrong with that? She should *want* to think about Sebastian. . . . He was still her boyfriend, even if her dad had forbidden her to see him. In a way, that made everything even more romantic and exciting. So why did seeing his name on her arm just make her more unhappy?

"Oooh, let's all sign Chelsea's cast!" Sienna cried from the other end of the deck, seeing what Sebastian was doing. Before she knew it, Chelsea was surrounded again, this time with people brandishing colored Sharpies. Soon her cast was a mess of smiley faces, names, flowers, animals, and cute little messages in every color of the rainbow. The whole time, Sebastian stayed at her side, a pleased smile on his face. She could tell everyone thought they were doing a great job of cheering her up. Too bad the only thing she could think of was the one person whose name was missing from the cast.

"Come on, Chelsea, time to go home," her dad said. Embarrassment washed through her as she turned quickly to see if anyone had heard her father speaking to her like she was a little kid. Most of the staff were busy clearing away the remains of the party, but Sebastian waved at her. He looked sad that she was leaving.

"Stay here," she mouthed to him when her dad

wasn't looking. Then she began following her parents down the gravel path.

"Oh no!" she said when they were halfway home.

Her mom turned, the branch of a pine tree throwing her face into shadow.

"What's wrong, honey?"

"Oh, nothing . . . I just left my sweater at the lodge," Chelsea said. "I'm going to run back and get it, okay?"

"Hurry home," her father warned.

"I will," Chelsea promised, turning and jogging back toward the lodge. The rest of the staff had gone, but Sebastian was still sitting in the wooden rocking chair that overlooked the lake, waiting obediently for her. She approached him silently, and he took her good hand, drawing her close. She could smell traces of lemonade and frosting on his breath as their lips met. He helped her onto his lap, wrapping his arms around her back and stroking her hair softly. Chelsea thought to herself that this was the perfect moment: quiet, romantic, forbidden. The two of them were alone with the dark resort and lake spread out before them, and she was nestled in his arms. Maybe it was the way her arm itched inside her cast that was making her feel tense and irritated instead of filled with passionate bliss.

"I'm sorry your arm hurts, Chelsea," he said, kissing her neck in a sexy way that made her toes curl inside her sneakers.

"Me, too," she whispered. "Let's make it stop."

She moved her face closer to his and looked into his eyes while she snaked her good hand under his shirt, exploring the warm, smooth skin of his chest with her fingertips.

"What can I do to make it better?" Sebastian asked. "What do you want?"

"I don't know," Chelsea sighed. What *did* she want? She wished she knew.

Sebastian cupped her chin in his hand and looked deeply into her eyes. "It will get better soon. I promise," he assured her before drawing her in for a long, sweet kiss.

Chelsea told herself that she was lucky to have Sebastian, that everything between them was perfect. So why couldn't she hurry up and fall in love with him already? Kissing him felt nice, even kind of sexy . . . but it didn't set off fireworks in her brain.

Sebastian bent to kiss her neck and Chelsea opened her eyes and looked out over the dark, silent lake. His words echoed in her head: *What do you want?*

Chapter Sixteen

Chelsea was going to kill the McCullough boys. From the moment Matt got a look at her cast, the prodding questions had started, and he hadn't let up since.

"If *you* broke your *arm* boarding, does that mean that Mikey's going to break *his* whole body?" Matt poked her in the side. They were sitting in the boat, watching as Mikey hung on to the towrope for dear life and tried to edge his little body in and out of the wake. Although Chelsea could tell that he was really nervous, he was actually doing a pretty good job. She was glad she'd separated them and let each one take turns behind the boat. Mikey seemed to gain a lot of confidence without his bullying brother around knocking him off the board.

The downside, of course, was that Chelsea had to keep Matt entertained.

"Are you going to kill my brother?" Matt demanded.

"Not before I kill you," Chelsea grumbled under her breath.

Matt heard her and whooped. "I'm gonna tell my dad you tried to kill both of us!" he shouted. "I'm gonna tell him you made us go boarding through shark-infested waters and wouldn't let us come back in the boat even after Mikey lost a leg!" The thought seemed to delight him as he leaned back, giggling uncontrollably.

"Mikey hasn't lost a leg," she pointed out, exasperated. She leaned over the side of the boat and called out to Mikey. "All right, I want you to try a little jump now. Go out of the wake, and when you edge back in—as soon as the nose of your board hits the white part of the water—just do a tiny little hop like this, okay?" She demonstrated by jumping in the boat, which rocked slightly from side to side.

"Augh! We're going to capsize!" Matt screamed. He pretended to be a news anchor talking into a microphone: "In a terrible tragedy on Lake Tahoe today, an evil, crippled wakeboarding instructor tried to murder two sweet boys by sinking their boat in shark-infested waters. The boys were saved by Superman, but Chelsea the evil wakeboarding instructor had her head bitten off by sharks." He laughed so hard at his own joke that he fell off the bench and went writhing around on the floor.

Chelsea rolled her eyes and looked out at Mike, who had edged so far out that he was having trouble getting back in. "Lean your body into it!" she called.

Mike looked scared. "I don't want to!" he yelled back. "How come Matt gets to hang out in the boat with you while I have to be out here on the water?"

Nina shot her a sympathetic glance from the driver's seat as Chelsea buried her face in her hands. If her arm hadn't been in a cast, she would have gone out there on her own board and shown Mike how to do it. It wasn't that hard, but it helped to see someone else demonstrate it first. Chelsea was at a loss. Teaching was hard enough, but teaching without getting in the water was turning out to be nearly impossible. Matt got up and tugged on the bottoms of her board shorts.

"What?" she growled.

Matt looked up at her with big blue eyes ringed in long black lashes. "Am I driving you nuts?" he asked sweetly.

"Yes," Chelsea told him.

Matt smiled happily and sat back down. "Good," he said.

*　　*　　*

Chelsea walked away from the boat feeling antsy and frustrated. Her arm itched inside her cast and she was dying to scratch it, but there was no way she could reach through the thick plaster.

The way her arm felt in her cast was the way she felt in her life: itchy and constricted. Summer was no good without being out on the water—without her long late-afternoon sessions in the boat. She missed the water and, more maddeningly, she missed Todd. He hadn't been around much, and she knew he was still mad about what she'd said to him after breaking her arm. She wished she could apologize—or, better yet, rewind to the moment right before she'd decided to try for a 720. He was right. She *had* been a stupid senseless daredevil and an idiot, and now she was paying for it. She wanted to tell him that, but there was no way she could. She was just too proud to admit that she'd been doing it to show off for him.

Instead, she wandered up to the tennis courts to see if Sebastian was done with his lesson. Lately, it seemed like Sebastian was the only person who could put up with her.

When she got to the terra-cotta tennis courts, Chelsea saw that Sebastian was still in the middle of a lesson. A tall, gawky pre-pubescent boy with his Adam's apple protruding almost as far as his nose and an over-sized purple T-shirt stood on the other side of the net, clutching a tennis racket like a caveman brandishing a club. His skinny legs spread out in a crouching stance as he waited for Sebastian to lob him the ball. But when the ball came to him, he flinched and swung frantically, like he was trying to swat a bee. It was obvious to Chelsea what the boy's problem was: He was terrified of the ball.

Sebastian vaulted over the net like a small, spry bird and was instantly at the boy's side. Chelsea laced her fingers through the tall fence surrounding the court and strained to hear what he was saying.

"Your stance is great, Francis." Sebastian's voice was soft and encouraging. "Your legs are in the perfect position, and you look like you're ready to swing the racket. But you can't wait for the ball to come to you. You have to be ready to smash it back before it's even over the net."

The boy nodded, looking anxious.

"You don't have to think of it as a tennis ball," Sebastian said. He smiled at the boy. "Who do you hate most in the world?"

It took Francis only a second. "Brett Carver," he said. "This guy in my school. He . . . well, never mind. He just sucks."

"Right." Sebastian went to the edge of the court and picked up the tennis ball, rolling it back and forth in his palm. "So this thing I am holding? This isn't a tennis ball—this is Brett Carver's head."

A slow, pleased look spread over Francis's face. *"Awesome!"* he said, now fully animated. His cheeks shone with eagerness. Chelsea watched Sebastian jump gracefully back over the net and serve the ball. This time the boy was ready, his eyes gleaming ferociously. He nailed the ball back with so much vigor that Sebastian had to leap to get it. Their game became a duet, the boy acting out his hatred against Brett Carver with Sebastian's quick, easy footwork as an encouraging backbeat. Chelsea couldn't help but be impressed at how naturally teaching came to Sebastian. It seemed like it was no problem for him to bond with his students rather than . . . well, threatening to kill them.

Chelsea thought to herself that Sebastian really was a great guy. She was lucky to have him. Maybe she really *was* starting to fall for him—even if she hadn't quite realized it yet. She leaned against the fence, trying to soak him up from afar. As she watched Sebastian, she had an epiphany. Suddenly she knew what she wanted: something only Sebastian could do.

At one point, Sebastian's eye caught Chelsea's and he winked sexily, holding up one finger to indicate that he'd be done in a minute. Then he lobbed the ball with just a tiny bit more force and follow-through than before, sending it flying over the boy's head and landing just inside the lines.

"Oh, man," Francis said as he jogged to get it. "I was really feeling that."

"Good!" Sebastian called jovially. "We'll pick it up again tomorrow. Remember for practice: When you serve, try moving your arm like this." He demonstrated a long, smooth follow-through, which the boy imitated. "Good. You're looking fantastic. See you tomorrow!"

"Bye," the boy said, jogging off the court.

Sebastian ran over to Chelsea and kissed her through the fence. "Hey, how was your lesson?"

"Not as good as yours," she answered, coming around the side of the fence and onto the court. "That kid Matt's a terror. Won't leave me alone."

"Ah," he chuckled. "The fun kind."

"What? You're nuts. I'm exhausted just *dealing* with him—let alone the actual teaching part. Plus, I don't even get to go out on the water," Chelsea explained, pouting.

"Poor baby." Sebastian draped an arm over her shoulder and kissed the tip of her nose. "I wish I could make you happy."

"You can." Chelsea kissed him back, fiercely, on the lips. "I need your help. I need to get back out on the water, Sebastian. It's all I want. I'm not made to sit around."

"I know." Sebastian's forehead was up against hers, his eyes still smiling. "That's one of the things I like about you." He raised his eyebrows flirtatiously. "You're feisty."

He said *feisty* like it was a cute thing. Maybe he didn't get it. She didn't want to be cute—she wanted to be the best. "Sebastian," she said, "if I still wanted to compete in the Challenge, would you help me?"

Sebastian's brow wrinkled. "But you can't compete," he said. "Your arm is in a cast. They wouldn't even let you."

"The cast is supposed to come off a few days before," Chelsea reminded him. "If I could just find a way to practice in the meantime—"

"You're not going to heal if you don't let your body rest," he said. "It's not good to practice with an injury. Every athlete knows that."

She *did* know that. But she couldn't respond. She felt herself choking up again, feeling the same panic she'd felt when she first woke up in the hospital. Sebastian seemed to see the pleading look in her eyes, because he put his hands on her shoulders and quietly kissed her forehead. But that wasn't what she wanted. She wanted so much more.

Chapter Seventeen

A ll right, Nina, let's go back to shore," Chelsea
instructed the driver. Carl, a beginner with so little
balance that she wasn't sure he would ever be able to
get up, let alone ride, had just climbed back into the
boat and was looking at her dejectedly through the
droplets of water on his eyelashes.

"Has it really been an hour already?" Nina asked. "It
feels like less."

"Of course," Chelsea assured her happily. "Time flies
when you're having fun."

"I wasn't really having . . . ," Nina began, but
stopped short when Chelsea shot her a death glare. "All
right, let's go in."

Nina gunned the motor on the boat, and Chelsea's

heart began to race as they headed back to shore. She felt bad about cutting Carl's lesson short by fifteen minutes, but she had more important things on her mind. She had a plan.

"Oh, look, Sebastian's here," Nina said as she pulled the boat into the dock. She shot Chelsea a knowing look. "Should I leave you two alone?"

Chelsea bristled. Did *everyone* at the resort know what she and Sebastian had been up to? As much as she tried to keep it quiet, Sebastian was always slipping his arm over her shoulders or trying to take her hand while other people were around.

Chelsea ignored Nina's insinuations and turned to Carl. "Good job," she told him. "We'll work on getting up on the board during your next lesson."

Carl climbed out of the boat, followed by Nina.

"See you later, Chelsea." Nina's voice had a sing-songy quality that set Chelsea on edge. "Have fun."

"Yeah, okay. Bye," Chelsea said, annoyed. Sebastian was already heading toward her.

"Why did you want me to meet you here?" he asked.

"Well, I thought since we both had some time off, we could take a little ride," Chelsea said, trying to sound casual and upbeat. "You know, someplace alone."

A big smile spread across Sebastian's face. "That sounds like a great idea," he replied, climbing into the boat and leaning in to kiss her on the cheek.

"Cool," Chelsea said. "Want to drive?"

Sebastian laughed. "I've never driven a boat before."

"But don't you want to learn?" Chelsea hoped she didn't sound too desperate. Teaching Sebastian to drive was all part of her plan. "It's just like driving a car."

"I guess I'm up for anything," Sebastian said easily.

Relief washed over Chelsea, and she impulsively wrapped her arms around him and kissed his cheek. "Awesome," she said. "I'll back it out for you and get us onto the lake. That's the hard part."

*   *   *

Once they were in the middle of the lake, Chelsea slowed the boat and switched seats with Sebastian. She showed him how to work the throttle, where the brake was, and how to speed up and slow down. "Generally, you want to keep the speed around twenty-two-and-a-half miles per hour," she told him. "Now, try to go around the island."

Sebastian pulled out the throttle and the boat surged forward, practically knocking Chelsea out of her seat. "Hey, easy!" she called. "These boats are sensitive. Maintain the right speed."

"All right, all right." Sebastian slowed down. Once he'd gotten them around to the other side of the island, Chelsea had him slow the boat until it came to a gentle stop, drifting slightly in the soft breeze rippling the lake's surface. Stillness filled the air, punctuated only by the sound of Jet Skis and laughter off in the distance. Chelsea leaned toward Sebastian and kissed him again. Smiling, he pulled her over and onto his lap. Chelsea opened her mouth and lightly touched her tongue to Sebastian's lower lip. He let out a soft moan and kissed her harder. When she pulled away, he was breathing heavily.

"Sebastian," she said, looking into his eyes, "I need you to help me with something."

"What?" he asked breathlessly. He reached for her again, but she laughed and leaned away from him.

"I *need* to compete in this Challenge," she said. "And I need to win. And if I'm going to win, I need to practice—and if I'm going to practice, I need someone to drive the boat."

"Oh." Understanding slowly dawned on his face.

Chelsea took his hand. "Please," she said, looking into his eyes.

"I don't know . . . ," he replied uncertainly. "I'm not sure this is a good idea."

"Sebastian." Chelsea tried to keep her voice calm, even though the inside of her brain seemed to be twisting in a million different directions. "I'm going crazy without the chance to ride, and the thought of skipping the Challenge is eating away at me. I feel like I can't be *me* without this, and you're the only one who can help me."

"Chelsea . . . ," Sebastian said helplessly.

She put both her arms around his neck and kissed it. She looked pleadingly into his eyes. "If you care about me, you'll do this," she said, inwardly cringing at her own words.

She could see the battle raging in his mind play out on his face. "Fine," he said finally. "I'll do it. But you have to promise me you'll be careful."

"Oh, thank you!" Chelsea pitched forward, hugged him, and planted a huge, happy kiss on his mouth.

Then she sat back again. "Sebastian, you really are an amazing boyfriend." And in that moment, she actually felt like it was true. She kissed him one more time before leaping to her feet. "So let's do this—I've got my board stashed under the seat."

*   *   *

Chelsea trudged to shore, her entire body aching from her session riding with Sebastian at the wheel. She had never realized how exhausting it could be to ride behind an inexperienced driver. In between all his false starts and varying speeds, Sebastian had caused her to take several inopportune dives into the frigid Tahoe water, and the few tricks she'd had the chance to attempt were thrown off by the weight of her cast.

Chelsea had begged off Sebastian's invitation to stay

in the boat and make out, claiming she was tired and needed to rest. But as she dragged herself toward home, she realized there was only one thing that could make her feel better: ice cream.

As she climbed into her beat-up old Jeep, she realized that she hadn't left Glitterlake's grounds since her accident. It was so easy to get caught up in the life of the resort and forget there was even a world outside. Going into town would be good for her, she hoped. At the very least, it would help get her mind off Sebastian and her most recent debacle on the lake.

Her mouth watered at the prospect of a fudge-sprinkle-dipped caramel swirl cone. Chelsea pulled into the gravel parking lot of the local ice-cream shop, Claire's Cones, and she was so preoccupied choosing between a sugar and a waffle cone that she didn't even notice the couple sharing a sundae at one of the store's five small tables. She had already paid for her cone and turned around to look for a seat when a pang in her stomach made her lose her appetite completely. Todd sat directly in front of her, feeding a large spoonful of dripping ice cream to a thin girl with aggressively high-lighted hair. The girl slurped it up suggestively, staring deep into Todd's eyes.

I have to get out of here, Chelsea thought. She was about to head toward the door when Todd looked up and noticed her.

"Hey, Little M," he said easily. He swirled his spoon in a pool of fudge sauce and smiled smugly. The girl he was with looked up, surprised to find her date talking to someone else.

"Gosh, what happened to your arm?" she asked.

"Wakeboarding accident," Todd told her without taking his eyes off Chelsea's face. "Unlike me, Chelsea doesn't always put safety first."

"Right." Chelsea's cheeks flared with embarrassment. "Well, I have to get going. Nice running into you."

Just then, the opening chords of Justin Timberlake's "SexyBack" came tinkling from inside Todd's date's beige Coach bag.

"Oh, that's Tina." She scooped out a sleek pink Razr and flipped it open, pressing it to her ear. "No, I'm out with Todd. Yeah . . ." She giggled. "*Again.* Listen, let me take you outside." She stood up and wiggled her fingers at Todd, who responded by blowing her a kiss. A wave of nausea rolled through Chelsea as the girl pushed open the door to the shop's wooden porch and continued her chat where she couldn't be heard. Todd returned his attention to Chelsea.

"What?" He had obviously noted her harsh glare, and he raised his voice a couple octaves as he mimicked her. "Nothing is going on between me and her. *Really* . . ."

"Screw you, Todd," Chelsea spat back at him before

storming out of the store. She realized she was shaking as she tossed her uneaten ice-cream cone in a nearby KEEP TAHOE CLEAN trash can, and as she peeled out of the parking lot, spraying gravel under the Jeep's tires, the last thing she noticed was the sliver of toned, tan stomach peeking out from between Todd's new girl's tank top and skintight Luella jeans. Everything about her exuded sex . . . in fact, when Chelsea thought about it, everything about *every* girl Todd dated exuded sex.

As she turned into the long winding driveway that led from the main road to Glitterlake's property, Chelsea wondered if all the sex-exuding, kittenish girls Todd dated actually *had* sex with him. Had he done it with that girl from the ice-cream store? With Vanessa? With any of the girls he had dated last year . . . or the year before? Maybe that was the reason all those girls seemed so much older and more sophisticated than her, even though some of them were her same age. Maybe that was the key. Maybe you couldn't be truly sexy without experiencing sex first.

As the lake appeared in a glimmering sweep of blue below her, Chelsea had a revelation. Maybe sex was the missing thing in her relationship with Sebastian. Could doing it unblock all the love for him she was sure she had stashed somewhere deep inside? She knew that having sex was something you should do only with someone you loved, so if she was even thinking about it, she must love him, right? The more she thought about it, the more she thought that there was only one way to find out.

But where should she even start? She parked and got out of her car, wishing as she entered her house that she had someone to talk to. She had lost count of all the times she'd heard groups of girls whispering and giggling about sex in the halls at school, and for the first time she wished she had a close-knit group of girlfriends to whom she could go for advice.

She climbed the stairs and wished, as she passed Sara's room, that she had been nicer to her half sister all summer. Sara would be the perfect person to talk to about something like this: She was older and wiser, and obviously had tons of experience with boys. Sara would know exactly what to do in her situation.

Chelsea realized that she had stopped in front of Sara's open door and was looking directly into the empty room; specifically, she was looking at the diary sitting on Sara's desk. The same trance that had overtaken her when she tried on Sara's clothes slipped over her again, and Chelsea found herself entering her older sister's room, picking up the diary, and letting it fall open to the first page.

If Chelsea couldn't talk to Sara directly, maybe she

could at least learn something from her journal. At that moment, nothing could have convinced Chelsea that Sara's diary didn't hold the key to everything there was to know about boys and sex. But what she read surprised her.

> *June 12*
> *Well, I finally managed to talk Mom into let-*
> *ting me stay with my real dad over the summer.*
> *Glitterlake Resort, here I come! It'll be great*
> *getting to know that side of my family better*
> *and getting some nature time, but mostly I just*
> *need to get away. I feel like everyone here knows*
> *and is laughing at me, and I just can't take it*
> *anymore. That, and every time I see him I feel*
> *like my heart is breaking all over again. How*
> *could I have been such a fool? I should have*
> *seen it all along.*

> *June 18*
> *My Goals for Summer:*
> *Read up on bio and chem so I'm fully prepared*
> *for Honors Botany*
> *Complete "Native Plants Guide" for Dad*
> *Make pressed-flower kit for Chelsea*
> *No boys!!!!*

June 29
Simon called again and I hung up on him. I
know he's just going to say he feels guilty about
the whole cheating thing and I know I'll get
sucked back in if I hear his voice again. Argh.
Guys. All they think about is sex anyway. I told
Leo about it, and he thinks I'm doing the right
thing. I kind of wonder if Leo is into me, but I
just don't want to ruin my first real friendship
with a guy.

A loud thud made Chelsea leap to her feet, shove
Sara's diary back into its spot on her desk, and race out
of the room. She had already flopped down on her own
bed, with the door shut safely behind her, when she
realized it was just the wind knocking a low pine branch
against a window. Still, she had read enough. Sara might
have been a lot less secure and a lot more tortured than
she came across, but one thing was clear to Chelsea.

If all guys thought about was sex, then she was definitely going to give Sebastian something to think
about . . . and she was going to do it as soon as possible. Before she lost her nerve.

Chapter Eighteen

Chelsea checked her watch for the millionth time in the ten minutes she'd been down at the dock. It was just past midnight, and a red half-moon hung low in the sky.

She rubbed her legs, which were beginning to get goose bumps from the cold, and she wished she'd opted for a pair of jeans instead of the baby blue Miss Sixty faux-cashmere shrug and white Forever21 minidress she'd chosen during her covert mall run. A twig snapped loudly on the path to the dock, and Chelsea nearly jumped out of dress, cast, and skin simultaneously. The thin beam of a flashlight played over her feet, and Sebastian's slight shape emerged from the shadowy woods. She sighed in relief, willing her heart to stop break-dancing in her chest.

"So what's so important that it requires a secret midnight meeting at the dock?" Sebastian asked, kissing her lightly on the lips.

"Just wanted to spend some quality time with you," Chelsea said mysteriously. "I have a special surprise planned."

She grabbed him by the shirt and pulled him toward her, feeling suddenly aggressive. She pressed her lips hard against his, kissing him more passionately than ever. When they broke apart, he finally looked at her outfit and smiled.

"Oh," he said shyly.

"You like it?" she asked, tugging at the hem nervously.

"It's very . . . short," Sebastian said.

"I know." Chelsea climbed into the boat. "That's the point. Are you getting in?"

Sebastian stood on the dock, looking at her with a cute but confused grin on his face. "Shouldn't you tell me where you're taking me first?"

"You'll like it," Chelsea said. "That's all you need to know."

"You're sure acting different tonight." Sebastian shrugged and joined her in the boat, smiling as he rubbed her knee.

Chelsea remembered slipping the small handwritten note telling him to meet her at the docks at midnight into his palm. She had felt reckless, daring, and sexy, like a bombshell spy in an old James Bond movie. When she'd looked up, she must have had a secret smile on her face because Todd gave her a *look* across the table and her smile had faltered and faded.

She wondered what Todd was thinking when he looked at her like that. These days, his unreadable looks were the only communication they had. They both sat at the staff table at meals and participated in the conversation, but they never directly addressed each other. Sometimes when she looked over at Todd, she thought she caught him quickly looking away, but she could never be sure.

Chelsea dragged her thoughts away from Todd by leaning over and giving Sebastian a kiss on the cheek. Then she started the boat and eased them out onto the still, dark waters of Lake Tahoe.

"Are you going to keep me in the dark all night?" Sebastian goaded her as they crossed the lake.

"All will be revealed soon enough," she replied cryptically.

"The island?" Sebastian asked as she docked. "Funny . . . nobody mentioned there was a party here. It must be *super* secret." His tone was light and jokey as he took her hand, but she was almost positive she could feel his pulse racing beneath his skin. What was *Sebastian* so scared of? He'd been to the island late at night for parties before, and he had *certainly* been alone with girls before. Maybe she was just imagining it? When she turned to look at him at the entrance to the Shag Shack, the smile on his face was as easy and good-natured as ever.

"Surprise!" she said, reaching up to switch on the Coleman lantern that dangled from a hook on the ceiling. The lantern gave off a low, steady glow and caused shadows to dance in the small wooden room as it swung back and forth. As their eyes adjusted to the light, Chelsea noticed that the lantern illuminated a little red cooler, an ancient cabinet that Chelsea knew contained a box of Trojans, some spare batteries for the lantern, and a long-abandoned box of Oreos. And in one corner was the infamous mattress, covered in a faded North Face sleeping bag.

"Wow," Sebastian said in a low voice, shaking his head and smiling with one side of his mouth. "Chelsea, you are a piece of work. You know that?"

"Um . . . thanks," she said, not quite knowing how to take that. "You want a beer?"

"Sure," Sebastian said, continuing to look around. Chelsea crouched by the cooler and removed a bottle for each of them. They sat side by side on the mattress, sipping slowly with their legs out in front of them. Chelsea's skin still speckled with goose bumps from the chilly night air.

"So . . . ," Sebastian began. But he didn't seem to know where to take that thought.

"I wanted us to have somewhere that we could be alone together," Chelsea said, feeling like she needed to explain. It had seemed like such a good idea as she'd formulated it in her head over the past few days. She'd imagined exactly how the night would unfurl, Sebastian's delight and surprise. She thought about the way that their bodies would move in the shadows of the lantern, in the small wooden shack that had seen other couples like them on so many other nights like this. She had thought that in the Shag Shack they would be far enough away from the resort not to have to worry about being caught and they could really let go and just be together. Finally that nagging voice in the back of her head would disappear and it would just feel *right*.

She hadn't counted on the awkwardness. Or the cold.

"You're shaking," Sebastian pointed out.

"It's chilly." She wondered if she sounded sexy at all or just inexperienced and dumb.

"Come on." Sebastian's voice was protective. "Let's get under the blanket. I don't want you to freeze."

Chelsea gratefully set her still-nearly-full beer on the floor and crawled under the sleeping bag, kicking off her flip-flops as she got in. Sebastian followed and wrapped his body around hers, cradling her head against his chest and pulling one of her legs between his. She huddled against him, listening to the rustling of noises outside the cabin, the steady rhythm of his breath on her cheek and the regular, comforting beat of his heart.

He kissed the top of her head, and then, when she raised her face to look up at him, he kissed her lips. Chelsea kissed him back, tentatively at first . . . and then more forcefully. She felt herself drifting far away from the tawdry mustiness of the Shag Shack, the pain and inconvenience of her broken arm, and the confusion that had been poking at her heart all summer. Sebastian's skin was soft and smooth under his shirt, and his hands exploring her body were strong and sure.

"Are you sure?" Sebastian asked before taking off her shrug and easing her dress off over her head, and she nodded, wanting him, unable to speak. There was a moment of awkwardness when the dress snagged on her cast and they both had to fumble to get it off, but then Sebastian started to laugh and she laughed with him and then their mouths came together again, fiercely covering the laughter and nerves.

Neither of them spoke when Chelsea reached into the small cabinet next to the mattress and handed Sebastian a condom. His eyes asked a question and hers answered and then they were both under the blanket again and she was so nervous and excited she could barely breathe. His body was between her legs, and she was half-delirious and half-shaking, thinking this was really it: She was really going to do it. She felt him pushing against her and raised her hips to meet him, and suddenly it started to feel really good—like nothing she had ever felt before. Chelsea heard a strange sound escape her lips. Her hands flailed and she heard a loud crack. She felt the dull thud in her bad arm as her cast connected with something in the air.

And then Sebastian was all the way over on the other side of the mattress. It happened so quickly that she didn't even know how he had gotten there.

"What happened?" Chelsea asked, feeling dizzy and confused. Had they just . . . done it?

"You just smacked me in the head with your cast," Sebastian said. "Hard."

"Oh, man." It went beyond embarrassment—it seemed like every cell in her body was trying to hide behind the others. She was totally mortified. "Sebastian, I am so sorry. Are you okay? Let me see."

He gingerly removed his hand, and she winced as she saw the bump on his head, already red and swelling to the size of a golf ball. "Does it hurt?"

"Yeah," Sebastian admitted. "Although . . ." A smile started to creep across his face.

"Although *what*?" Chelsea nearly screamed. "Are you okay? Do you have a concussion? How many fingers am I holding up?"

Sebastian's smile turned to giggles as he pushed

Chelsea's hand to the side. "You have to admit, that was pretty funny, Chels."

"Oh, God. That was so *not* funny!" Chelsea insisted, hiding her face in her hands. "That was *so* embarrassing!" But as she thought about it, she couldn't help starting to giggle, too.

Sebastian cracked up again. "It gives new meaning to 'Not tonight, dear . . . I have a headache.'"

Chelsea snorted, collapsing on the mattress in a fit of laughter.

"Oh, man . . ." Sebastian fell on top of her. "How am I going to explain this? What if your dad asks what happened to my forehead?"

"Tennis accident?" Chelsea suggested.

"We'll be dubbed the most accident-prone couple ever," Sebastian mused.

"Probably because we *are*," Chelsea said. "Or at least I am. Jeez."

"It's all right." He kissed her sweetly. "You're wonderful."

"Here," Chelsea said, scooping ice from the cooler and wrapping it in one of his socks. "Put this on your forehead until we get home."

"Thanks."

"Sure." Chelsea cuddled up next to him under the covers, wondering what had just happened. She felt tired all of a sudden.

After a while of just lying there together, Chelsea started shivering.

"You're cold," Sebastian murmured, stroking her good arm. "Let's get you home."

Silently they got up, put on their clothes, and slipped back into the boat. The moon was now down toward the edge of the horizon as they pushed back out onto the lake.

Chapter Nineteen

Slow down!" Chelsea screamed, hanging on to the towrope for dear life with her one good hand while waving her cast frantically in the air. The plastic bag she'd wrapped around it to keep her cast dry caught in the breeze and crackled. She struggled to retain her balance, sighing to herself as the boat slowed. "Please maintain speed!" she shouted to Sebastian, although she wasn't sure he could hear her over the roaring wind.

Chelsea leaned too far to one side to compensate for the extra weight of the cast. *I'll just try for a simple 360*, she thought. *I won't even try any inverts—that would be nearly impossible with this thing on my arm.*

She had just started to edge in when the boat surged

forward with a newfound burst of speed, almost sending her hurtling into the foamy white water of the
wake.

"Hey!" she yelled. This was her third practice session
with Sebastian: the third time Nina had given her a sus-
picious smirk when she cut the lesson short and
Sebastian met her by the dock, and the third time she
had to deal with the fact that Sebastian still couldn't get
the hang of driving the boat. Varying the speed wasn't
just annoying—it was dangerous. She knew he wasn't
doing it on purpose, but it made practicing nearly
impossible. Not that it would have been a breeze even
with Nina or Todd—the weight of her cast made it difficult to balance, and the fact that her arm ached underneath didn't exactly help matters.

She shook her cast angrily in the air and saw
Sebastian smile sheepishly in the rearview mirror as he
brought the speed back down. Chelsea went in for the
360 but lost her balance in the middle and found herself
sprawled out in the lake a second later, cold water lap-
ping at her face and seeping in through a gash in the
plastic bag wrapped around her cast.

"Damn!" she screamed as she swam clumsily toward
the boat, trying to keep her bad arm above the lake's
surface. She climbed into the boat to find Sebastian suppressing a grin.

"What are *you* smirking about?" she asked grumpily.

"Nothing," Sebastian said, snorting laughter through the hand he'd clapped over his mouth.

"No, what?" she insisted.

"It's just . . ." Sebastian's eyes danced. "We had this cat at home, and one day she jumped into the bathtub not realizing it was full of water, and the expression on her face—well, that's what you look like right now."

"Shut up," Chelsea snapped, playfully smacking him on the arm with her good hand. The water seeping into her cast was making her skin itch so much, she wished she could crawl right out of it. She ripped the plastic bag off her arm and reached across Sebastian to grab a towel. As she leaned over him, he caught her by the shoulder and brought her face down to his for a gentle kiss. "You're adorable when you're angry," he told her.

"Stop," Chelsea huffed. "I don't want to be adorable. I want to be *good*." She shook him off and grabbed the towel, rubbing ferociously at her stringy wet hair.

"You *are* good," Sebastian tried to assure her.

"Oh, shut up, I am not," Chelsea said. "And you're not helping any with your driving skills—or should I say lack thereof."

"Hey!" Sebastian sounded genuinely angry for the first time since she'd known him. "I'm doing you a huge favor. I'm putting *your* health and *my* job at risk, and the least you could do is thank me. I didn't think this was a good idea in the first place, and now I'm starting to think that it just plain sucks."

"You don't understand," Chelsea snapped, knowing she was being obnoxious, but beyond the point of caring. "You don't know what it's like to want something this bad. I mean, you *gave up* a competitive career to teach—how could I expect you to know what I'm going through?"

Sebastian's eyes flashed. "You are being mean and ungrateful," he said. "And I really don't appreciate it."

Chelsea knew that she was being unreasonable, but she couldn't stop. Everything was wrong, and for once Sebastian wasn't making anything better.

"Forget it, Sebastian!" she said. "I don't need your help." She leapt onto the dock and began running up the gravel path away from the boat. Sebastian and the memory of her whole botched attempt at wakeboarding bobbed in the shallow water and seemed to be mocking her as she ran away.

As Chelsea ran, her breath grew short and ragged and her eyes began to burn. When she ran past a tourist family strolling lazily toward the lake, they turned to look at her, mouths and eyes gaping open in surprise. But Chelsea didn't stop. She had to get away. To get somewhere she could be alone.

The path curved through the rear buildings of the resort and turned to dirt at the base of the mountains.

The ambient resort noises faded behind her until all she could hear was the twittering of birds, the burbling of a stream, and her own uneven breathing. A canopy of leaves blocked out the sunlight as she veered off the path and toward the stream. Her face felt like it was on fire, and she squatted on a large flat rock by the water, scooping handfuls of it onto her burning cheeks.

It wasn't until her chest heaved and she let out a loud sob that Chelsea realized she was crying. She *hated* crying! And that just made her cry even harder.

She felt like she couldn't do anything right anymore, and her life was just falling to pieces. She had lost the ability to do the one thing she was good at, and all the competitive spirit she could muster wasn't sharpening her ability to perform with an injury one bit. What if her parents did find out? Not only would she be dead meat, but she'd be letting them down once again.

But if she couldn't wakeboard, what would she do? It was bad enough that her parents, whenever they weren't yelling at her for doing something wrong, were acting like she barely existed and like Sara was the best thing to ever happen to Glitterlake.

It was bad enough that, ever since the incident with Sebastian in the Shag Shack, she hadn't been able to decide if she was still a virgin or not . . . and that either way, thinking about it made her feel kind of slimy. Being around Sebastian had gotten pretty weird, and the fact that he was always treating her like a gentle, delicate flower was starting to get on her nerves. Ever since they had done it . . . or not done it . . . or whatever . . . he had taken kind of a protective stance toward her and was always telling her she was "adorable." It was the kind of attention she'd thought she wanted, but now that she had it, she wasn't so sure.

Chelsea's body continued to convulse with sobs as the thoughts rolled through her mind in long, confused waves. She couldn't remember the last time she had cried for so long or so hard. It felt like all the emotion she had bottled up over the past year was pouring out, and there was no way to stop it. And the weird thing was that it actually felt kind of good.

I miss Todd, Chelsea thought, sniffling loudly. The thought lodged itself in her head, crowding out all the others as she pictured Todd expertly driving a boat as she clung to the towrope, Todd smiling at her in the late afternoon sunlight right after they had docked; Todd's lean, spare wakeboarding style. She missed more than just boarding and competing with him, though: She missed talking and joking with him, and the way he looked at her, and the way her heart fluttered in her chest every time he did.

I still have it pretty bad, she realized miserably, launching into a fresh volley of tears. Her whole relationship with Sebastian, even finally maybe-sorta-kinda having sex with him, hadn't made her want Todd any less. And now it was too late for there to be anything between them—even friendship.

Chelsea sat on the rock and cried her eyes out until the sun had stopped sending dappled patterns through the trees overhead and the air had grown chilly and dark.

It seemed like she would cry forever, but finally the tears stopped and Chelsea picked herself up and went home.

Chapter Twenty

Chelsea could hardly believe she was actually going to the Keep Tahoe Blue Gala with a date. She had been attending the annual fund-raiser for the League to Save Lake Tahoe every year for as long as she could remember, first with her parents and then with whichever summer staffers found themselves without summer loves by mid-August, but this was her first time ever going with a guy . . . or wearing a dress that cost more than her competition-only wetsuit.

She reminded herself that Sebastian was worth it. After their fight he had found her and apologized, even giving her a small bouquet of wildflowers he had picked himself. To her surprise, she found herself not only accepting his apology (and his kisses) with open arms, but asking him to be her date for the dance as well. And she had even told her father that she was taking him. Surprisingly, he hadn't argued. Maybe, despite the occasional nagging doubts that lingered in the back of her mind, she still had a chance of falling in love with Sebastian. And her father would somehow accept him.

Chelsea took a break from rearranging her wallet, lip gloss, and car keys in her tiny black satin clutch to stare one more time at her reflection in the mirror. The slinky royal-blue halter dress draped low on her back and clung to her legs, making them appear sky-high in her black patent leather Steve Madden peep-toe pumps. She had to admit that she looked fantastic . . . well, at least from the neck down. Her face and hair were another matter entirely. She had carefully followed the directions for "smoldering evening eyes" and the "classic starlet up-sweep" on teenglamour.com, but even after several passes at each, she was pretty sure she looked more like a raccoon with a Mohawk than a glamorous diva with smoky eyes.

She frowned as she reached for her Neutrogena makeup remover pads, which were half gone even though she had just bought the package that afternoon.

Someone knocked softly on her door as she was wiping at the deep black liner ringing her eyes.

"Who is it?" Chelsea prayed it wasn't Sebastian. He

had said to meet him at the main lodge, but thanks to her continuous makeup disaster, she was running late.

"It's Sara," the voice at the door said.

"Come in." The door cracked open and Sara appeared, looking more perfect than ever in a '50s retro-looking baby blue dress with white polka dots and amazing red patent leather heels. Chelsea felt a wave of jealousy when she looked at Sara's expertly waved retro hair and dewy, fresh makeup, accented with a shade of lipstick that matched her shoes.

"I was just coming to see if you needed a ride," Sara said. "I'm leaving as soon as Leo gets here."

"Thanks, but it'll take me forever to get these eyes right," Chelsea said.

Sara squinted at Chelsea's reflection in the mirror, trying not to smile. "Let me guess . . . you went for smoldering and ended up looking like a raccoon?"

Chelsea couldn't help laughing. "Like five times now. How did you know?"

Sara laughed. "Been there. I can help, if you want."

"Really? That would be amazing." Sara suddenly seemed less like the too-perfect older sister who had been stealing her spotlight all summer and more like an angel of mercy sent to help her just in her time of need. Chelsea felt a stab of guilt. Why had she spent all summer snooping around in Sara's things and giving her the cold shoulder?

"It's really no problem." Sara pulled up Chelsea's desk chair and rolled over to her, reaching for something in the pile of brand-new makeup crowding her vanity. "The secret is to do it mostly with shadow, not eyeliner. The liner's too dark and it smudges easily, which is what gives you the raccoon-eye look. Close your eyes, okay?"

Chelsea did as her half sister asked, and the room slipped into a semi-awkward silence. "So you're going to the gala with Leo?" Chelsea asked, just to say something.

"Yeah, but only just as friends," Sara said, sliding something cool and damp over her upper lids. "I know he'll make me laugh the whole time."

Chelsea recalled Sara's diary entry and wondered if there was anything helpful she could say without giving away what she'd seen.

"Open your eyes," Sara instructed. Chelsea turned slowly to face the mirror—and nearly squealed with delight. Sara had somehow transformed her face from "Ashley Olsen after a bender" to "Ashley Judd at a premiere." Even her irises seemed to have a twinkling, come-hither look.

"Wow," Chelsea said, her mouth hanging open in shock. She shook her head. "This is . . . amazing."

"Thanks," Sara said, looking down bashfully. "If you want, I can do your hair, too."

"That would be great," Chelsea said. She watched

Sara's reflection in the mirror as her sister began removing pins and brushing out her hair. "Seriously, Sara, you're great at this."

"Oh, it's just something I learned to do," Sara replied. "I used to go out a lot."

"You're lucky," Chelsea said.

"Eh. It gets old after a while," Sara said. She didn't sound very happy, and Chelsea couldn't figure out why. She would do *anything* to have guys pay as much attention to her as they did to Sara. Her half sister clearly didn't know how good she had it.

"You're lucky to have Sebastian," Sara said, twisting Chelsea's hair into the style she'd been struggling with for hours with just one easy flip. "He's nice, and he's obviously crazy about you. It's not easy finding a guy like that."

Another wave of guilt rolled through Chelsea. She couldn't believe she'd just been thinking about how annoying Sebastian could be. "Leo's great, too," she offered.

Sara sighed. "Leo is *just* a friend," she reminded Chelsea. "And a friend is *all* I want right now. I am officially taking a break from boys this summer."

And I'm just waking up to them, Chelsea thought.

She was about to ask Sara more, but was interrupted by her phone beeping to tell her she had a text message.

At lodge, the text from Sebastian said. *Where r u?*

"Wow, I'm totally late," Chelsea said. "I better run and meet Sebastian."

"Do *not* run in those heels," Sara cautioned, and they both laughed.

"Hey, Sara," Chelsea said as she hurried toward the door. "Thanks for fixing my hair and face."

"No problem," Sara said. "Thanks for listening to me rant about guys."

"Anytime—and that was hardly ranting." Chelsea threw her wrap around her shoulders. She headed out into the night air feeling sultry and glamorous . . . and thinking that maybe having Sara around the resort wasn't so bad after all.

* * *

As Chelsea ascended the steps of Ponderosa Manor, the sprawling Victorian mansion where the Keep Tahoe Blue Gala was held each year, she felt like she was walking into a fairy tale. The stately porch was adorned with thousands of tiny blue Christmas lights that twinkled like stars, and she could already hear strains of music and laughter coming from inside.

Sebastian offered her his arm as they made their way through the sumptuous lobby with its velvet wingback chairs, large potted ferns, and sweeping mahogany staircase. When they reached the entrance to the ballroom, an actual butler in a tuxedo helped Chelsea off with her wrap and whisked it away.

"Wow," Sebastian breathed as they entered the ballroom. "These people really know how to throw a party!"

The large parquet-floored ballroom glimmered in the subtle light of the crystal chandeliers overhead. Long blue candles burned in candelabras that reflected against the floor-to-ceiling windows, and tea lights floated in water bowls, illuminating the blue balloons and silver streamers strung festively about. A band played onstage on one side of the room, and a table piled high with punch bowls, crystal goblets, and dainty finger foods occupied the other. Most impressive about the ball, though, were the partygoers: a selection of the Tahoe region's wealthiest and most influential families, from resort and casino owners to old money dating back to the gold mining days, all the men in dapper evening jackets, and all the women wearing gowns in various hues of blue in honor of the lake that had brought them all together.

"Why, Chelsea McCormick!" Deirdre LaClaire, chairwoman of the gala, exclaimed, rushing up to them. "Don't you look fabulous! But whatever happened to your arm? Wakeboarding accident, I suppose—you daredevil, you! You know, I practically didn't recognize you. You look about twenty-five and like you just stepped off the pages of *Vogue*. And *who* is this young man you're with?"

Deirdre's double chin wiggled as she reached out to take Sebastian's hand. Sebastian brought it to his lips as he introduced himself, and Mrs. LaClaire nearly melted into a puddle of royal blue sequins at his feet.

"I've known her since I was a little kid," Chelsea whispered to him after Deirdre had waddled off. "I'm not supposed to know this, but she and her husband are some of Glitterlake's key investors."

"Ah," said Sebastian. "Well, she's right: You do look like you just stepped out of *Vogue*. In fact, you look better. I'm glad I'm your date."

"Thanks," Chelsea said, forcing herself to smile at the compliment. She knew it was supposed to make her happy, but for some reason it just made her feel anxious and slightly oppressed. *Why can't I just appreciate him more?* she wondered.

"Want to dance?" Sebastian asked. He took her hand and led her to the middle of the dance floor, where several couples and a gaggle of preteen girls were already moving to the beat. Chelsea was pleased to discover that, as long as Sebastian held on to her hand, she actually felt okay dancing in her new heels. *Maybe I can sort of get into this,* she thought, looking around the room.

After returning Sebastian's encouraging smile, Chelsea scanned the room for people she knew. She saw Sara in a corner by one of the candelabras, laughing at something Leo was saying, with one hand on his shoulder. And over by the punch bowl Mel and Sienna were talking with two handsome, yuppie L.A. types who had probably flown in to play around on Jet Skis for the weekend. She even saw her parents circling the dance floor, her mom's arms around her dad's neck and her upturned face alive and happy in the sparkling light from the chandelier overhead.

Sebastian turned slightly, giving her a view of the long bank of floor-to-ceiling windows on the ballroom's east side. Her eyes skipped over a sea of faces and stopped on one that was staring directly at her: Todd. Before she had a chance to slide her gaze away, they had locked eyes, and her heart jumped. He looked more devastatingly gorgeous than ever in a simple navy blazer and light blue shirt that brought out the mountain-lake hue of his eyes, and his gaze seemed to be punching her in the stomach.

"Are you okay?" Sebastian's asked, his breath warm and moist in her ear. "You just made the strangest face."

"I'm fine," Chelsea lied as Todd finally looked away and down at the floor.

Sebastian pressed in closer to her. "Sure?" he repeated.

"Positive," Chelsea said, her voice sounding fake even to her. Not that it mattered . . . all she'd done was *look* at Todd. Last she'd checked, looking at someone wasn't wrong or illegal. Even if it *did* make her body feel like it was made out of syrup.

"Want to take a break?" Sebastian asked. "You don't seem very into dancing right now."

"That would be great," Chelsea replied with relief. She glanced back toward Todd—he was staring at her again! Her throat went dry.

Sebastian took her arm and they began heading toward the punch bowl—only to be waylaid by Deirdre LaClaire, wobbling toward them with her BFF and gala co-chair Nadine Monteague in tow.

"Oh, just the young man I was looking for!" Deirdre squealed, grasping Sebastian by the arm. His mouth widened in surprise, then closed quickly into a gracious smile. "Sebastian, you simply *must* meet my dear friend Nadine. Nadine, Sebastian here is a tennis instructor . . . *from Brazil*. Sebastian, darling, I wanted to talk to you about perhaps teaching a private clinic just for Nadine and myself. . . ."

Chelsea tuned out as Deirdre went on. Her throat was so dry, it hurt. She gently touched Sebastian on the shoulder.

"Sorry to interrupt," she said, trying for her best apologetic smile. "I'll just be over at the drinks table if you need me, okay?"

Sebastian kissed her cheek haphazardly, clearly engrossed in whatever Deirdre & Co. were plotting, and Chelsea picked her way through the sea of dancers to the relatively safe haven of the drinks table. She gratefully ladled herself a goblet full of pale pink punch garnished with clouds of creamy sherbet and turned away from the table, intending to find a quiet corner. Instead, she found herself face-to-face with Todd.

"What are you, following me?" She hoped her words were strong enough to cover up her trembling.

"Hardly," Todd snorted. "What's your deal?"

"What's my deal?" Chelsea's voice rose with hysteria and several heads in their immediate vicinity swiveled to stare. "Can we talk outside?" she hissed.

Without speaking, Todd grabbed her arm and practically dragged her out onto the balcony. Twinkling lights festooned the grand columns and stars twinkled in the clear sky overhead, but Chelsea and Todd were too focused on their argument to notice.

"So?" Chelsea asked casually, breaking free. "What do you want?"

"*Excuse* me?" Todd asked, getting in her face. "It's more like what do *you* want!"

It was the same question Sebastian had asked her on the lodge's porch nearly a month ago. But instead of making her sad and confused, hearing it from Todd just made her mad. "What do *I* want? I want to know why you keep looking at me like that. Why can't you just leave me alone?"

"I'm not looking at you," he answered, turning his head to stare angrily over the edge of the balcony.

"So, what, I'm just making it up?" Chelsea could hear herself getting loud, but she couldn't help it. He was doing this on purpose to drive her crazy. And it was working. Instinctively, she reached up and turned his face so that he was looking at her. "You've been giving me the evil eye all night. I just . . . I just want to know what the hell you want from me."

They stared at each other for a long moment in silence. Todd's eyes were dark, and he looked like he was biting the insides of his mouth to keep from saying something.

"So?" Chelsea prodded. "What do you want from me?"

As she watched Todd's face constrict with rage, she shivered. It was freezing out. And they were locked in a death glare. Todd's eyes seemed to be growing larger and larger, and she realized suddenly that it was because his face was moving closer to hers. She couldn't understand why . . . until suddenly his lips were on hers.

For a long moment, Chelsea was too surprised to move. And then she felt her mouth melting into Todd's, her arms wrapping around his neck as if they had always belonged there, her hands stroking his hair the way they had longed to do all summer. There were fireworks, singing birds, bolts of lightning: the works. It was simply the most amazing moment she had ever experienced in her life, and she never wanted it to end.

But then it did. The universe, which had shrunk to

include only her and Todd during their kiss, expanded rapidly, and she blinked, looking around. That's when she saw Sebastian standing at the edge of the doorway, his face paler than she'd ever seen it. Had he seen them? And did it matter?

She turned back to Todd. "I . . . ," she began. But what could she possibly say? That she'd been waiting her whole life for this moment, but the timing wasn't right? "I have to go," she whispered.

Todd's face clouded over again before he turned around and sauntered off as though nothing had happened.

Chelsea ran over to Sebastian.

"What was *that* all about?" Sebastian's voice was colder than the lake in January.

"You saw." Chelsea felt dizzy. The world dipped for a moment, then righted itself again.

"Oh yeah," Sebastian sneered. "I saw. You two-timing . . ." He muttered something in Portuguese.

"I'm so sorry, Sebastian," Chelsea gulped. "I didn't even realize I still liked Todd until just now. That was the first time we ever kissed, I swear."

"I know." Sebastian looked past her into the darkness, refusing to meet her gaze. His voice was tinged with resignation and regret. "I could tell from watching you. And I could see that you would never feel the way about me that you do about him."

A piece of Chelsea's heart broke off. She was filled with regret as she looked at Sebastian. He was so cute and had been so sweet to her . . . and yet, it hadn't been enough. "It's not that I don't like you, Sebastian," she began. "I do. I just . . . I guess I didn't really know what I wanted."

It was hard for her even to say the words out loud. Up until this summer, she had always known exactly what she wanted and thought that she was basically a good person. Now she felt horrible: like a user, someone who only took what she wanted and didn't care about anyone else.

"Save it." Anger had replaced the regret in his voice. "You really played me, Chelsea. I guess this is what I get for actually caring." He brushed past her and stalked off into the darkness, leaving her alone and shivering on the cold, dark porch.

Chapter Twenty-one

The buzzing in Chelsea's ears grew to a dull roar as Sebastian hurried away from her and into the night. She took a deep breath and the night air rushed into her lungs in a fresh, cool burst of jasmine and pine, making her shiver. She rubbed her arms to warm up, remembering that she had given her wrap to the butler, and looked around at the other people on the veranda, couples and small groups talking softly together in the shadows, holding wineglasses that glinted like jewels in the twinkling blue lights.

The lobby provided a welcome gust of warmth and bustle: the groups larger, the laughter sharper, the wineglasses fuller. Chelsea suddenly felt overwhelmed and sank into one of the plush velvet wing chairs by the fireplace, partially obscured by a large fern. She felt strange and guilty and worried about Sebastian. How could she have just let him go that easily when he had been so kind and attentive to her all summer? She felt too guilty over using him to figure out what she wanted.

But, to Chelsea's surprise, she was also relieved. She didn't have to spend any more time wondering why she couldn't appreciate the guy she was with and why she was longing for the one she didn't have. As dark and painful as her confrontation with Sebastian had been, she knew she had done the right thing.

A gentle peal of laughter pierced her reverie. "Todd, that's so funny!" said an unfamiliar voice through the giggles.

"Thanks." The response was definitely Todd's voice. Chelsea's body stiffened and her throat closed up, making it impossible for her to breathe. Trying to move as little as possible, she peeked around the edge of the potted fern and saw Todd sauntering toward the stairs, his arm draped casually over the shoulder of a short, busty blonde in a very expensive-looking low-cut dress. Chelsea had never seen her before, but the girl's radiant smile slashed at her heart.

Nausea clawed at Chelsea's stomach as Todd touched the girl's arm.

"I'm staying upstairs." The girl flirtatiously dangled a

hotel key in front of Todd's face. "Want to . . . see my room?"

"Uh . . . sure," Todd replied. The room spun and all the color and noise ran together in one big, messy swirl, like paint being rinsed down a drain. Chelsea struggled to keep her body still so she wouldn't give away her hiding place. The blonde started up the stairs, playfully tugging at Todd's arm.

Chelsea literally started to gag. She felt her stomach rising in her throat and bolted out of her chair, stumbling through the too-bright, too-loud, too-stuffy lobby and out into the night air once again. Clutching her stomach, Chelsea bent double over the porch railing and heaved.

*   *   *

Chelsea felt like a cold thin hand was reaching into her stomach and yanking out everything she'd eaten for the past week. When it was finally over she was still bent double, gasping for breath and swabbing miserably at her mouth with the back of her good hand as tears of humiliation stung her eyes. She was too embarrassed to look around and see if anyone had noticed, and she still felt too weak to move. All she wanted was to drink a big glass of water, take off her stupid slinky dress and painful heels, and crawl into bed and die.

She thought maybe she would just stay right there on the dark corner of the veranda forever when she felt a small hand on her back.

"Are you all right?" Sara's soft, concerned voice asked.

Chelsea turned slowly and saw her sister blanch slightly at the sight of her pallid skin and running eyes.

"Chelsea, what's wrong?" Sara caught sight of the mess in the bushes. "Did you have too much to drink?"

Chelsea made a noise that sounded like a drain unclogging, and Sara immediately held out her arms, letting her dive into them and quietly cry against her shoulder. She didn't say anything about Chelsea ruining her dress but just held her and stroked her back and made comforting little cooing noises as Chelsea heaved and snuffled.

"Did you have too much of the champagne punch?" Sara asked when Chelsea was finally calm enough to pull away. "It can really sneak up on you if you're not careful."

Chelsea shook her head. "I only drank from the non-alcoholic punch bowl. I was afraid if I got tipsy in these heels, I'd break my other arm."

Sara laughed lightly, but a moment later her nose wrinkled with worry. "Do you think you have food poisoning?" she asked. "The shrimp cocktail seemed cooked enough to me, but I don't know, if you got a bad one—"

"It's not that," Chelsea hiccupped. Suddenly, the image of Todd and the blond girl ascending the staircase flashed in front of her eyes, and her stomach cramped up again. She dived for the railing and heaved, but nothing came up.

"Chels, I'm really worried," Sara said. "What's wrong?"

"Nothing," Chelsea mumbled, turning around. She sank slowly to the floor, hugging her knees without caring if her new dress got dirty.

"People do *not* vomit into bushes over nothing," Sara pointed out.

It was true. What had just happened with her and Sebastian and Todd and the blond girl wasn't nothing—it was enough to make her physically ill, and it was a whole big secret that she'd been bottling up inside herself all summer long. Chelsea was tired of dealing with it all on her own and wondering if she was crazy for feeling the way she did. She realized that she *wanted* to tell someone, someone who would understand. And Sara was sitting right there on the porch floor next to her, apparently not caring if she got her dress dirty, either.

"It was over a boy," Chelsea said quietly.

Sara's eyes widened and her hands flew to her mouth. "Oh no—did something happen between you and Sebastian?"

Chelsea nodded grimly. "But it wasn't just Sebastian," she added. "I mean, we got in a fight and broke up and—"

"Oh, I'm so sorry," Sara said sympathetically. "I just can't imagine it. He always seemed so into you."

"He didn't dump me," Chelsea corrected her. "I dumped him."

"But why?" Sara seemed genuinely confused.

"Because I like someone else," Chelsea began. It felt good just to say it—not because it was something she was proud of, but because it had all been inside her head for so long. Words tumbled out of her mouth as she launched into the whole story: how she had liked Todd ever since she was fourteen, their wakeboarding rivalry and all his hookups with tourist girls, and how even though she had thought hooking up with Sebastian would make her forget about Todd, it only made wanting him that much worse.

Sara's china blue eyes grew almost as round as grapefruits when Chelsea got to the part about seeing Todd with the bimbo in the hotel lobby, and she put a sympathetic hand on her knee.

"No wonder you were puking in the bushes." She rubbed her hand back and forth. "I would have done the same thing."

"So I'm not a total freak for being this crazy about someone I'm not even dating?"

"No," Sara assured her. "Love makes everyone

emotional. It can make you excited, depressed, and exhausted—and that's just when you're in a relationship! And then finding out the person you want to be with has been with someone else: Well, it's literally enough to make you sick."

Chelsea leaned her head back against the porch railing and looked up at the stars. The gentle night breeze was finally starting to cool the burning in her cheeks and forehead.

"If it makes you feel any better," Sara ventured, "I don't know Todd well, but maybe all those girls he runs around with are just substitutes for who he really wants to be with."

"Who's that?" Chelsea asked.

"You," Sara said. "I've seen the way he looks at you, Chels. It's different from how he looks at any of those other girls. Maybe he's just afraid to admit that he wants to be with someone who could beat him at his own game."

As much as Chelsea wanted to believe her, she just couldn't. Didn't Todd realize by now that if he wanted her, he could have her?

"Thanks, Sara," Chelsea said. "But I'm pretty sure it's not true. If Todd liked me, we'd be together by now."

"You'd be surprised how backwards guys can be with their emotions," Sara replied, smiling a little. "Sometimes you have to beat them over the head with what they want. Other times, you have to just sit back and wait for them to come to you. And the problem is, you can never tell the freakin' difference."

Chelsea sighed and closed her eyes. It was all too much. The whole night—no, the whole *summer*—had been so up and down that it was no wonder she was feeling nauseated. Every move she made was the wrong one. All her instincts had been out of whack. She had thought Sara was some man-eater out to sabotage her whole family, and instead it turned out she was just nice. And normal. And . . . well, *really* nice.

Chelsea took a deep breath. "I have something to tell you," she said before she lost her nerve. "When you first got here, I really didn't like you. But I was also really jealous because you seemed to be getting all the attention and all the guys, and those are always things I've secretly wanted, without even realizing that I wanted them. And I didn't think I could talk to you, because I thought you didn't like me—"

"That's not true!" Sara interjected, but Chelsea held up a hand to stop her. She wasn't done yet.

"I did some things I shouldn't have," Chelsea blurted out. "I went into your room and tried on your clothes and I borrowed a skirt and got a stain on it and I overheard part of this phone conversation you had with Simon once and then this one time I was really desperate for guy advice and I read your diary and . . . look, I know it's wrong, but I just wanted to know and I didn't have anyone to go to and . . ." She trailed off.

Sara was staring at her, her mouth hanging open in shock. "You *read* my *diary*?"

More tears welled up in the back of Chelsea's throat. "I'm so sorry," she whimpered as they spilled out over her cheeks. "I was just so confused."

"If you wanted guy advice, you could have just *asked* me," Sara said. "That's what sisters are supposed to be for."

"But I never thought of you as my sister," Chelsea admitted. "Until now."

Sara sighed and held out her arms. "Come here." She patted Chelsea's head as her little sister cried into her shoulder. "I know what it's like not to know who to turn to for advice, so I'll forgive you this once. But don't you *ever* read my diary again."

"I won't," Chelsea sniffled.

"Good." Sara stood up and held out her hand to help Chelsea to her feet. "You must be exhausted. I'll take you home."

Chapter Twenty-two

The aggressively blue skies and cheery yellow sun the next day were a sharp contrast to Chelsea's pensive gray mood. Even though Sara had gotten her home and into bed before midnight, she had spent most of the night tossing, turning, and sweating through her sheets. She had turned the evening's events over and over in her mind, feeling angry about Todd and worried about Sebastian, pleased but weirded out by her new friendship with Sara, and alternately proud of and disgusted with herself.

Get over yourself, the sun seemed to say as she picked her way down the gravel path leading to the tennis courts. At the same time, a boat soaring through the dazzling lake seemed to nudge her on, telling her she was doing the right thing.

As she got closer to the tennis courts, she could see two figures volleying the ball back and forth. One was taller and more awkward than the other, who was dark and graceful, moving with the fluidity of a dancer. His movements flowed from his hips, and his racket seemed like an extension of his arm as he hit the ball in a smooth arc over the net.

The other player, although he lacked Sebastian's grace, was holding his own on his side of the court. He raced back and forth to return Sebastian's serves, hitting the ball with short, almost angry bursts of power. Chelsea watched Sebastian's movements slow and grow more laconic as his partner continued to run and dive for balls. Finally, in a quick swoop of triumph, Sebastian's opponent landed the ball before Sebastian had a chance to dive for it, and he raised his arms in victory.

"Great game, Francis," Sebastian said as Chelsea approached the court. "You've improved a lot this summer. I'm proud of you."

"Yeah, well . . . it's mostly thanks to you," Francis said, his shoulders hunching gawkily. "You're a good teacher, man."

"You're good at tennis," Sebastian said, his voice open and genuine. "You should keep practicing when you go home."

"I think I will," Francis said. "I never thought I'd say

this—I mean, I only took these lessons because my mom wanted me to—but I really like it."

"Excellent," Sebastian replied, giving Francis a high five. "And if you ever have questions or if you just want to talk or anything, you have my e-mail."

"Thanks," Francis said, turning and jogging off, his feet never seeming to leave the ground.

Chelsea felt a twinge of regret. Sebastian was hot, and a really good guy, and *much* better at teaching than she would ever be. Maybe she had been stupid to dump him. But she knew in her heart that there was no way she'd ever be able to feel the way about him that she did about Todd. She just hoped that he would be able to forgive her. Squaring her shoulders, she called his name.

Sebastian turned slowly, and his face darkened. "What do you want?" he asked.

Chelsea realized she was nervous. She had been up half the night trying to figure out what to say to Sebastian to make things okay, but now that he was actually in front of her, she couldn't remember any of the speech she'd planned.

"I, uh . . . thought I owed you an explanation." Her throat was suddenly tight and dry.

"You explained enough last night." Sebastian clutched his racket more tightly as he approached. But despite the harshness of his words, his tone wasn't angry. He just seemed resigned.

"No, I didn't," Chelsea insisted, lacing her fingers through the fence as Sebastian came around to the other side. "I didn't tell you how great I think you are. You've been *amazing* to me. You were so sweet this summer and you taught me about . . . well . . . about guys and stuff. Because before I met you, I had, like, zero experience with guys."

She watched his eyebrows rise in surprise and pressed on. "Seriously, Sebastian—I'd barely ever kissed a guy, let alone dated one. And you were so nice and patient and—"

"Chelsea," Sebastian interrupted her. "I had no idea. You were so poised and confident when it came to physical stuff. Like that night in the Shag Shack—"

Her cheeks grew hot. "That was my first time," she said. "Well, if it even counts as a 'time.'"

Sebastian laughed. "Mine, too," he said, leaning against the fence. "And I can't figure out if it counts, either."

This time it was Chelsea's turn to be surprised. "But you act like you have tons of experience with girls," she said. "You're all passionate and romantic—and you're such a good kisser!"

Sebastian shrugged and smiled boyishly. "At home, I'm just a tennis geek," he admitted. "I spent most of my life training and competing before I realized it wasn't for me. The way I acted this summer? I was just acting like the rich, confident men who bring women to the country club where I worked in Rio. I never really had a girlfriend. That's partly why I wanted to date you—I thought a strong, self-assured girl would be good for me."

Chelsea couldn't believe it. "You mean we had each other fooled all along?"

"I guess so," Sebastian agreed. "You were a good girl-friend, Chelsea."

"You're not mad at me?" Chelsea asked.

Sebastian shook his head. "Not mad," he said. "A lit-tle sad. I would have liked to spend the last few days here with you. But it would have ended anyway. And even if it's ending now, it was still pretty good."

"Thanks," Chelsea said, taking his hand. "I think so, too."

Sebastian leaned forward and kissed her gently, chastely on the lips. "You'll always be my maybe-first, Chelsea," he said. "Now do what you gotta do. I'm root-ing for you."

* * *

"Okay, I want you to both listen very carefully," Chelsea said to the McCullough boys, who sat facing her in the boat in the middle of the lake, each of them eagerly clutching a board in his hands.

"I can't listen carefully," Matt complained. "I have ADHD. It means I can't sit still ever, even for a second."

"Well, that's why you're about to get in the water and pretend you're being chased by a giant bloodthirsty shark," Chelsea explained.

Both boys' eyes lit up. "They're not real sharks, are they?" Mikey asked worriedly.

"No, stoopid," Matt huffed, elbowing his brother in the ribs.

Chelsea glared at him. "Of course they're not real sharks," she said gently to Mikey. "There are no sharks in Lake Tahoe—only fish. But today, we're going to pretend there are. So, Matt—listen to me, Matt!" she cried, grabbing him by the back of his life jacket as he attempted to moon a passing tour boat.

Matt wriggled in his seat and stared up at her with his long-lashed cupid eyes.

"There are sharks out there," she said, leaning in as if she were telling them a juicy secret. "They're swimming back and forth across the wake like this." She indicated snaking motions with her good hand. "And you always have to stay away from them. But there's a shark in the wake, too! So when you get to the wake, you have to bend your knees and hop so you leap over the shark's head."

The boys looked at her with round, excited eyes. "Coooool," they breathed in unison.

"Ready?" Chelsea asked Matt.

"Yeah!" Matt said. He raced to the edge of the boat and was about to lower himself into the water when he turned around to face Chelsea. There was something in his face she had never seen before: uncertainty.

"What's wrong?" she asked.

"Uhm," Matt said. He sounded embarrassed. "Uh . . . there's not *really* sharks in the water, is there?"

"No, don't be a baby!" Mikey screamed, clearly delighted at the opportunity to turn the tables on his bullying brother.

Matt's lower lip set in a hard line. "Fine," he said, and jumped off the boat. Mike and Chelsea watched him swim out and turn around, wobbling a little on the getup but quickly straightening himself.

"Go wide," Chelsea shouted over the noise of the boat's motor as she watched Matt drift away from the wake. "Okay, now there's a shark chasing you! Quick, come in!" Matt cut in again, and when he was almost to the wake she cried, "Shark!" Matt looked surprised for a moment, but bent his knees and leapt, almost making it all the way over the wake.

"Good job! Now the next time you come in, the shark is even bigger—so you have to jump higher and clear the whole wake."

"Otherwise you're shark meat!" Mikey shrieked gleefully. As Matt approached the wake a second time, they both screamed, "Big shark!" together, and he went soaring across the wake, landing with a wobble—but still on his feet—on the other side. Mikey and Chelsea cheered, and even from the boat, she could see that Matt had a huge grin on his face.

Chelsea smiled to herself. It might have been nearly the end of summer, but she was finally starting to get this whole teaching thing down.

Chapter Twenty-three

Chelsea sat tensely on the contestants' bench, sweat pouring down her back so that her best competition wetsuit clung to her body even though she hadn't even gotten in the water yet. All around her, the resort was bustling with color and noise: Bright advertisements from the Challenge's sponsors covered every inch of the metal bleachers set up along the lakeshore, announcements blared over loudspeakers, motorboats sputtered to life, and the deeply tanned, visor-bedecked crowd chattered excitedly in the stands.

The chaos had descended on the resort the morning before as contestants, fans, reporters, and their friends and family began arriving in droves. They backed up traffic on the long winding driveway and clogged the lobby with their overstuffed luggage and loud voices, occupying every room and cabin to bursting.

Chelsea's parents were ecstatic—business had never been so good! But as she ran around helping her parents with the extra workload, Chelsea was also keeping an eye on the influx and beginning to get very, very nervous. Her arm had just come out of the cast a few days before and still felt very weak. Everyone had been telling her all summer that she'd be crazy to still do the Challenge after her injury, and she was finally starting to believe them. Plus, there was the tiny matter of not having told her parents yet that she was competing. Chelsea knew that as soon as they called her name over the loudspeaker, she was in for it.

"Monica Kaplan!" boomed the loudspeaker, and Chelsea watched the small freckled girl with spiky blond hair give her boat driver the signal to go. Chelsea sat forward on her seat. Monica was a relative newcomer to the competitive wakeboarding world, but she already had a formidable reputation as a force to be reckoned with.

Monica got up quickly and cut through the water like a Japanese fighting fish in her aqua-and-neon-pink wetsuit. Her first series of jumps was quick, light, and precise; Chelsea could see that the hype around her was well-deserved. It had been that way with many of the women who had gone before, too: They were simply better than Chelsea had expected.

Don't think that way, she told herself sternly. *You still have a couple of tricks in your back pocket that you haven't seen a single one of them do.*

Monica executed a brilliant backflip with a surprising twist right at the end, followed by a series of quick surface turns that made her look more like a ballerina doing pirouettes than someone hanging on to a rope behind a speeding motorboat. At the end of her routine, the crowd in the stands broke into raucous applause and catcalls. Chelsea turned and saw that many of the spectators had gotten to their feet to give Monica a standing ovation. Sweat drenched the small of Chelsea's back as the tiny doubt that had been there since the morning before blossomed.

She tried to clear her mind by running through her routine in her head, but got distracted as Monica's scores blasted out over the speakers: 43.26, 39.51, 39.69, 44.87, 40.04. They were the highest scores yet in their division. Chelsea began chewing on the insides of her cheeks.

Monica returned to the bench, her pale cheeks flushed. Droplets of water shimmered in her still-spiky hair.

"Good job out there," Chelsea congratulated her with grudging admiration. "You looked great."

"Thanks!" Monica seemed genuinely pleased. "You're up next?"

Chelsea nodded through what seemed like buckets of sweat pouring from every gland in her body. She felt like she might hyperventilate.

"Good luck, then," Monica said, reaching out to give her a high five.

At that moment Chelsea heard her own name screaming through the distortion of the speakers. She took a deep breath, got up, and headed for the boat.

"Ready?" the driver asked as she strapped her feet into the bindings on her board.

"Ready as I'll ever be," she replied, striving for a cheerful tone. The truth was, as nervous as Chelsea felt, just being near the water made her feel a little bit calmer. She knew that no matter what happened, she was doing what she was meant to do.

"Let's do this!" the driver said, starting the motor. Chelsea's head didn't even have a chance to stop spinning before she was in the water and swimming out to the full length of the rope behind the boat. In those brief moments of buoyancy, her head cleared and she found herself entirely focused on the task at hand.

Chelsea quickly became a combination of animal and machine, with the sleek strength of a panther as well as the speed and precision of an electrical conduit. She flew through her first series of moves. Her mind raced mere moments ahead of her body as she calculated the weight and velocity of each jump and turn.

She could hear the crowd *ooh* and *aah* as she landed, and the sound boosted her courage. She had the rare and spectacular feeling of flying on the water, as if she had grown wings and her feet weren't touching anything at all. Going into her grand finale, she knew she was going to hit it out of the park.

She braced herself as she was about to go into her final trick—the one that nobody had ever seen her perform successfully before, but that she knew deep in her heart she could do.

She gathered every ounce of strength that she had and threw herself into the jump. She felt her body hurtle through the air once, twice, and . . .

She reached for the water with her toes, bending her knees in preparation for her landing. But the water wasn't below her feet where she thought it was going to be. She had only a second to panic before she landed smack on her butt, the towrope slack in her hands.

A loud, pained gasp went up from the bleachers, and Chelsea realized in horror that she had blown it. A landing like that could take ten points off your score if the judges were feeling generous—and those ten points were enough to land her soundly behind Monica, and probably everyone else.

As she swam back to the boat, her body felt as old and unwieldy as the rock-topped mountains ringing the lake. She knew that as soon as she stepped onto dry land she would have to stop grumbling and smear a big fake smile on her face. And, sure enough, there was the ESPN3 reporter with his microphone, an even bigger and faker smile stretching his square, tan face. He was surrounded by reporters from lesser local and sports papers, as well as a cameraman and someone dangling a boom mike right in Chelsea's face.

"Chelsea McCormick," he crooned in his sports-caster drawl. "That was some move you tried there. How do you feel after that baaaad digger?"

Chelsea's grin felt fragile, like it would shatter at any moment and give way to tears. "It's too bad I wiped out at the last moment, but I feel like I gave it my best shot and I'm proud of myself anyway," she lied, not wanting to sound like the sore loser she actually was.

"You sure did, you sure did," the anchor agreed. "Not many sixteen-year-old girls have attempted a seven-twenty in competition—and certainly not so soon after recovering from a broken arm. How does that make you feel?"

How was she even supposed to answer something like that? She stared into the camera for what seemed like an eternity, watching the anchor's smile strain until it was really more of a grimace. "Well," she finally said, "I like challenges, and this was definitely a chal-lenge."

"Well, it sure was, it sure was!" he replied heartily,

laughing more in relief than because he thought what she had said was particularly funny or true. "Hey, it sounds like they're announcing your scores."

Chelsea held her breath while the numbers crackled in huge sound waves around her head. She was definitely way below Monica—in fact, thanks to that landing, she was now closer to the bottom than the top of her division. She wanted to weep.

"Well, that's tough luck, now, isn't it?" The reporter patted her on the shoulder with his huge ham of a hand. "But I bet you'll do better next year, right?"

"Of course." Chelsea stared levelly into the camera and tried her hardest to smile. "There's always room for improvement."

*　　*　　*

Chelsea watched the rest of the Junior Women's Division in a daze, her eyes glazed over. She berated herself as she watched other girls with less skill perform far easier routines than she had and still get higher scores.

She wondered if she was doomed to a lifetime of "almosts." She had almost nailed the routine, almost had sex with Sebastian, almost made friends with her half sister, and *almost* gotten Todd to notice that she could be more than just a boarding buddy. Everything was almost there, but not quite. She was becoming deeply, existentially tired of *almost*. Just once, she wanted things to be perfect.

"Still brooding over that landing?" Chelsea blinked to clear the haze in her head and saw Todd standing in front of her.

"No," she said.

"Liar." Todd plopped into the empty spot next to her. "I know you're playing it over and over in your head, thinking about how you could have done it better . . . and probably wondering what kind of score you would have got if you'd only done a five-forty instead."

"How'd you know?" Chelsea asked.

Todd shrugged. "You're Chelsea," he said simply. "That's what you do. You obsess over how you should have done everything better."

"Well, I should have," she replied, surprised that Todd knew her that well. "If I hadn't overcompensated on that last jump, I'd be a shoo-in for first place right now."

Todd's nose was wrinkled in confusion. "Why are you like that?" he asked. "It's one thing to want to be good, but you always push yourself *so hard*, like you have to be the best or it's nothing at all. I want to win, too, but there's something really intense about how competitive you get."

"Why am I so competitive?" Chelsea asked in disbelief. "Why do I always push myself so hard? Because I *have to* be the best, that's why! I have to win so I can prove that

I'm better than you." Chelsea clamped her hand over her mouth, shocked to hear the words even though she had long known them to be true.

The furrows on Todd's face deepened. "But you know you're better than me," he said quietly. "And I do, too."

Despite the staticky roar of loudspeaker announcements and the crowd, that moment felt silent to Chelsea. Silent, and suspended in midair like a wave still swelling before crashing into the shore.

"Do you really mean that?" she asked finally.

"Yeah," Todd said. "And most of the time, it kills me knowing it. I knew you were going to be good—probably better than me—from the first lesson I gave you. It hasn't been easy, Chelsea. But you're the best, and you deserve to win."

With that, he got up and began walking away. "Wait!" Chelsea called after him. Her mind was still somewhere back on *you're better than me*.

Todd turned and looked at her, the expression on his face one of both pain and triumph. "What?" he asked.

"Where are you going?" she asked.

"To resign from the finals," Todd told her. "I can't compete knowing you're the one who deserves to win."

"Todd, what? Wait!" Chelsea called after him. But if Todd heard her this time, he didn't turn around. Her head spun and her chest felt empty and cold. Todd had just given her what she always wanted. Why did it still feel like it wasn't enough?

Chapter Twenty-four

Chelsea had never felt so worn down. Every step of the way home seemed to require more than she had in her, and the tourists, spectators, and contestants spilling all over the resort only seemed to mock her failure. She kept her head down and one hand over her face, as if trying to block her eyes from the sun, so that nobody would stop her to comment on her routine on the way home. She knew she had failed. She didn't need the rest of the world reminding her.

The screen door of her family's log house slammed behind her as she entered, and she was halfway to the fridge in the kitchen when a large, heavy hand clamped down on her shoulder. She looked up to see her parents glaring down at her. She gulped hard. She knew what was about to hit the fan.

"We need to talk," Mark McCormick growled. "Sit."

Chelsea edged guiltily into one of the polished oak chairs surrounding the round kitchen table, feeling like a bad kid who'd been sent to the principal's office.

Her mom sighed and put her hand on her cheek. "Oh, Chelsea," she said, taking a seat next to her husband.

Chelsea sat in silence, waiting for it.

"So," her dad began. "We couldn't help noticing you competing out there. Care to explain?"

"I just had to," Chelsea said quietly. She didn't know why she hadn't just told her parents earlier—after all, they had to find out eventually. The event was held off their resort's beach, and it wasn't like they weren't going to show up.

"Against the doctor's orders? And ours?" her mom asked.

"Yeah," Chelsea said, gnawing at the skin around her pinky nail the way she did when she was very, very nervous. "I just couldn't bear the thought of not competing in the Challenge. You know how hard I worked and practiced all year, and how much this means to me. Suddenly not being able to do it was like having this big, empty black hole in my life, and it was just killing me." Passion and panic rose in Chelsea's voice. "I know you guys care about me and want me to be safe, but this Challenge has been my life for the past year: Everything

I've done has been working toward it. I knew I probably wouldn't win, but I had to compete. I just *had* to!"

"Chelsea," her mom said warily.

But her dad was smiling. He reached out and gently ruffled her hair. "You can be so stubborn, Champ," he chuckled. "Just like me. I remember how much my parents wanted me to be a lawyer like my dad. . . but the only thing I was interested in was travel. He practically disowned me when I took out a bank loan to open my first resort instead of enrolling in law school."

"Exactly!" Chelsea jumped in. "Look, I understand if I'm in trouble. I expect it! But I had to be true to myself and do the one thing I wanted to do most in the world."

"You are certainly in trouble," her dad replied. "Your mother and I need to discuss an appropriate punishment, but I can assure you that your actions will have consequences."

Chelsea looked down at the linoleum floor. "I just wanted to make you proud," she said quietly.

"Oh, honey," her mom said. "You make us proud every day."

"Really?" Chelsea asked, suddenly serious. She couldn't believe her parents would say that even after all the trouble she'd gotten into with the pool party, and then her accident, the constant sneaking around with Sebastian, and her forbidden participation in the Challenge.

"Of course," her dad assured her. "Did you ever think we weren't proud of everything that you've accomplished?"

"Well . . . sometimes I doubt it a little," she admitted.

"Having Sara here must have been a real change for you," her mom said, reading her mind the way only a parent could.

"It was different," Chelsea replied. "Sometimes I felt like no matter what I did, it would never be as good as Sara, and . . . oh, I don't know. . . ."

"The way we treated Sara this summer has nothing to do with either of you being as good as the other," Mark explained. "She's my daughter, too, but I barely know her. I have to make up for all those years of not really being there, and that means that your mom and I have to not only get to know her, but convince her that she's important to us. You already know you're important to us. Don't you?"

"Yeah," Chelsea admitted. She had always known that her parents loved and cared about her . . . but it still felt good to hear them say it. "I like having Sara here, too," she said. "It took me a while, but now I think she's pretty great. I'm glad she's part of our family."

"Good," her dad said in his no-nonsense way. "I know that sixteen is a little late to gain a sister, so I'm glad you're handling it okay. Then again, I don't know if you've ever met anything you couldn't handle. And honey? I'm sorry about Sebastian. I was completely wrong about him."

"Thanks, Dad." Chelsea smiled, hiding the sharp stab she felt in her heart. "So, um . . . can I have a sandwich now?" she asked. "Because I'm starving."

She leapt up and began rummaging frantically in the fridge for peanut butter—but not without giving each of her parents a big fat hug.

*   *   *

After the long, hot shower she'd promised herself, Chelsea rubbed Tiger Balm into her calves and shoulders, which were always sorer after a competition than after any practice session. Then she curled up in bed, hoping for a long, deep sleep to erase the memory of the fatal wipeout. But as soon as she was under the covers, Chelsea felt wide awake. Even as the sky outside grew darker and she forced herself to close her eyes and take deep breaths, she could hear snippets of live music and raucous laughter coming from the party down at the lake.

There's no point in going down there, she told herself sternly. *You'll just have to deal with everyone's sympathy, and Todd is probably hooking up with some chick this very minute.*

But despite everything, Chelsea had to admit that the party sounded like fun. Maybe she could just go down there for a little while and check it out . . . if it turned out to be lame, all she had to do was turn around and leave.

She pulled on her favorite olive-green Puma track pants and matching hoodie, slipped into her Reefs, and pulled her hair into a muss-free ponytail. At the last second, she added a lace-trimmed camisole underneath the sweatshirt for just a tiny feminine touch.

The strains of Phunky Chicken, a local funk band, grew stronger as she made her way down to the dock. As she drew closer, she saw that the judges' stand had been converted to a stage and the bleachers cleared away to make room for a temporary wooden dance floor, which was already occupied by a dense thicket of moving bodies. Paper lanterns dangling above the crowd glowed festively, and the makeshift wooden tiki bar in the corner was doing a brisk business handing out bottles of Jones Soda and Sierra Nevada, the Challenge's beverage sponsors.

"What'll it be?" the bartender asked as she approached.

"Root beer, thanks," Chelsea said. As he slipped the icy cool bottle into her hands, the bartender did a double take, and his face widened into a smile. "Hey, you're Chelsea McCormick!" he said. "That was one sweet routine out there. I can't believe you nailed all those gnarly tricks with your arm fresh out of a friggin' cast! You got bigger *cojones* than most of the guys out there!"

Chelsea's cheeks reddened at the compliment. But she was also confused. Why hadn't he mentioned the wipeout?

Not feeling quite ready to hit the dance floor, she took a seat at a table, sipping her soda and surveying the crowd. She saw Mel and Sienna dancing with two Australian guys who had competed in the men's division, caught a glimpse of her dad talking animatedly with the Challenge's head organizer, and waved to Sebastian and Nina, who were laughing together on the dance floor.

She was about to get up and join them when Monica Kaplan, wearing a Puma tracksuit almost exactly like hers, only in lavender, emerged from the crowd and slid into the seat next to her.

Chelsea reached out to slap her outstretched hand. "Congratulations on winning the division."

"Thanks." Monica smiled. "But I wouldn't have stood a chance if you'd landed that last jump."

"Oh, I don't know if that's true," Chelsea said. "You were awesome—you have great style, and you nailed every trick perfectly."

"Yeah, but I don't have the same gonzo do-it-or-die energy as you," Monica insisted. "You're like a wild animal out there. I can tell there's nothing you won't do—you'll probably be landing ten-eighties by the time you're twenty. You are *seriously* talented."

Chelsea was blown away. "But what about that digger at the end?" she asked incredulously.

Monica waved her hand dismissively. "Who even *tries* seven-twenties? That's what I mean—you're nuts out there, but you're amazing. Hey, I gotta go find my little brother—I promised I wouldn't leave him alone for too long. See you around."

After she had left, Chelsea stayed at the table. She tried to wrap her mind around the fact that Monica Kaplan, who had been dubbed the newcomer of the season by *Wakefiend* magazine, had just gone to such great lengths to compliment her. The Challenge was turning out to be full of surprises after all.

Chelsea finished her root beer and decided to hit the dance floor. As she floated through the crowd of dancers, she spotted Sara, who was laughing and beckoning to her. "Hey, come dance with us!" she called, and Chelsea joined her. Sara's face glowed with sweat and happiness—her hair was loose around her face, and even though she was wearing jeans, a T-shirt, and sneakers, Chelsea thought she looked prettier than ever. There was a new kind of twinkle in her eye, and Chelsea wondered where it came from.

It didn't take her long to find out. As they danced, Chelsea watched Leo spin Sara around. Laughing, Sara bent her head toward Leo's and gave him a long, passionate kiss on the lips. When they finally pulled apart, Sara's cheeks were flushed with pleasure and she was smiling wider than ever before.

"I thought you said you and Leo were just friends!" Chelsea whispered in her sister's ear.

Sara just shrugged and grinned. "I thought we were, too, practically all summer," she said. "But it turns out there was more there. I spent all summer taking a break from boys, and it turns out that Leo was spending all summer trying to teach me that they're not *all* bad, after all."

"Listen to that," Leo said proudly. "Apparently, I'm a catch. Who knew?"

"Oh, stop." Sara swatted playfully at his chest. Leo caught her hands and brought them to his lips.

"Wow." Chelsea was genuinely happy for Sara, but at the same time, seeing her sister and Leo together left an empty, aching hole of envy in her stomach. Everyone else had someone to share things with, and she was alone. As always.

The thought made her weary and sad. "I'm going to take a little break," she told the happy couple. "See you guys later."

She weaved in and out of the gyrating bodies until she was at the edge of the dance floor, and surveyed the partygoers clustered together at the tables around the edge. Suddenly, it seemed like everyone was part of a couple. Mel and Sienna had each taken their respective

Aussies to a different table—Mel's guy had his arm around her, and Sienna's was holding her hand. Even Chelsea's parents stood side by side as they chatted with the bartender, her mother naturally leaning into the curve of her father's side.

Chelsea was about to leave when she saw a familiar head of dirty-blond hair wandering away from the party, toward the lake. She sprang into action, following him down the winding gravel path, watching his tall, broad frame cross through the shadows of towering pines.

The dock creaked slightly as he stepped onto it, and when she followed a moment later the cool lake breeze caressed her face, washing away any traces of sweat left from her stint on the dance floor. Empty boats bobbed gently up and down like sleeping ducks, and the music and laughter of the party were faint sounds in the distance.

"Todd." Chelsea called his name softly, and he whirled around to face her.

"Did you follow me here?" he asked accusingly.

"Yes." Chelsea slowly approached him until she was close enough to see the uncertainty in his eyes. "I wanted to ask you something."

"Shoot," Todd commanded.

She wiped her sweaty palms on her track pants. "Why did you drop out of the competition today?" she asked.

Todd's blue eyes were dark against the night sky. "I

wanted to win that Challenge," he said. "But it wouldn't have felt fair. You're my real competition, and you always will be."

"Is that all you'll ever see me as?" Chelsea's voice shook. "The competition?" Tears quivered in the corners of her eyes. It wasn't fair that all he wanted was to beat her, when she wanted so much more.

"No." Todd shook his head, his eyes flickering with pain. "I *do* see you as more. And that scares the hell out of me. How are we supposed to be competitors and also . . . also . . ."

"Also this?" Chelsea asked. She took a step toward him, placed her hands on his shoulders, and brought her lips to his. At that moment, she could have sworn that the dock lifted into the air and started floating high above the lake, so far up that she could have touched the moon. Todd's soft, strong lips moved against hers, and he pressed her tightly to his chest, his heart beating a mile a minute against hers.

"Also that." Todd laughed slightly as they pulled apart, his arms still around her waist. "That's exactly what I'm talking about."

"I don't know how we're supposed to be competitors and also that," Chelsea admitted. "But I know it's what I've always wanted."

And then Todd said what were to Chelsea the two most beautiful words in the English language: "Me too."

She wrapped her arms around him even tighter and snuggled into his chest. Neither of them said anything else for a long time after that. Just holding Todd, smelling him, and listening to him breathe was enough. Chelsea had won the one thing she'd wanted the most, and standing there on the dock with her arms wrapped around the one person she had always felt she belonged with was the best prize in the world.

Chapter Twenty-five

There was always something bittersweet about the last day of the summer season. All the tourists were gone, and the summer staffers were running around packing all their things, cleaning out the barracks, and getting ready for the Last Afternoon Picnic that had been a Glitterlake tradition for as long as Chelsea could remember.

Chelsea sat on Sara's bed, watching her carefully fold her clothes into a huge suitcase.

"I'm sure going to miss your wardrobe," Chelsea joked.

"I knew it—you just love me for my clothes." Sara pretended to be insulted.

"Clothes, boy advice, and general sisterly there-ness," Chelsea checked off on her fingers.

Sara looked up from packing shoes in a garment bag and flashed a smile. "If you need help with any of those things, I'm just a phone call away."

"I may very well take you up on that." Chelsea fiddled with the corner of Sara's quilt. "So are you and Leo going to do the long-distance thing?"

"No." Sara laughed incredulously. "He's moving to Santa Cruz to be with me while I go to school. He's already hooked up a bartending gig there! Can you believe it?"

"Wow." Chelsea slowly let the news sink in. "He must like you a lot if he's willing to give up a season on the slopes."

Sara shrugged happily as she folded a cardigan into her suitcase. "He says he's always wanted to work on his surfing."

"Hey, girls," Patty McCormick called from downstairs. "The picnic is about to start—do you want to head down there?"

Sara grinned at Chelsea. "Good," she said. "I am ridiculously hungry."

The two of them thundered down the stairs, and Patty grinned at them, obviously happy to see they were finally getting along. She put an arm around each girl and they headed down to the beach, where most of the summer staffers had already gathered and were chowing down on hamburgers, hot dogs, and shish kebabs.

"All right, I know you're all busy eating, but it wouldn't be the end of the summer if I didn't give my famous end-of-summer speech." Mark McCormick got up on a picnic table and stamped his foot to get everyone's attention.

"Then don't give it!" Leo called out, and the entire staff laughed.

"Sorry, but a resort owner's gotta do what a resort owner's gotta do," Mark said jovially. "So, here goes . . . as I'm sure you all know, it's been a benchmark summer here at Glitterlake: from the resounding success of Sara's nature hikes to hosting the Northwest Extreme Water Sports Challenge. And of course, I can't help mentioning a certain not-quite-off-the-radar pool party"—many of the staff members giggled—"and all the great free hard manual labor I got as a result: That Breakneck Ridge Trail looks awesome!" At this, the entire staff burst into full-blown laughter, and Chelsea's father joined them.

"In all seriousness," he continued, "you did a stellar job this year, and thanks to you, Glitterlake had a better summer season than ever. I wish you all the best of luck in the coming year, and hope that you choose to spend next summer right here at home with your Glitterlake family."

Chelsea looked around and noticed that several of the staffers were actually getting misty-eyed. She felt sad herself: sad that summer was over, sad that Todd was going away just when they had finally realized their true feelings for each other, sad that wakeboarding season would soon be done, and sad that the resort would empty out and she would have to wait until the first snow brought all the tourists back for ski season.

"And now I want you to enjoy the rest of this beautiful afternoon," Mark said. "The tourists are gone, and the resort is your playground until you have to leave. Enjoy . . . and make sure you come and say good-bye to me and Patty before you leave!"

The end of his speech was met with thunderous applause. As the staff slowly rose and began to mingle, Chelsea found herself hurrying over to Sebastian.

"I know you're leaving for the airport in a couple of hours, and I wanted to make sure I got a chance to say good-bye," she said.

"I'm glad you did," Sebastian replied. He held out his arms and wrapped her in a huge, friendly hug. "I'm glad I met you."

"Me, too," Chelsea said. "Are you coming back next summer?"

"If your dad will have me," Sebastian joked, releasing Chelsea and planting a kiss on her cheek. "You take care of yourself while I'm gone, okay? No more broken bones."

"None, I promise," Chelsea laughed. She took off in search of Mel and Sienna, but Todd waylaid her. He was wearing his wetsuit.

"How about one last run before the season is over?" He leaned over to give her a kiss, and Chelsea's head swam with joy. Todd was kissing her in public! He was willing to let the world know that they were together!

"You know I could never say no." Chelsea grinned.

Ten minutes later she was zipping along behind the boat, the sun on her face and the cool Lake Tahoe breeze whipping through her hair. She could feel the energy of all the summer staffers on the shore: people she finally felt comfortable with, who finally seemed like her friends. She felt freer and happier than she had all summer. She was where she wanted to be, but she was also *who* she wanted to be: a strong, kick-ass girl who was, nevertheless, a *girl*, and who was comfortable enough with herself to land the guy of her dreams.

She maneuvered far out of the wake and began to edge in again, gathering the speed and momentum she would need to hurl her body into the air. As she did, she glanced toward the boat. Todd looked back at her in the rearview mirror and sensed exactly what she was doing. He quickly brought the boat around in a double-up, causing the wake to swell to twice its normal size before Chelsea launched herself in the air on her board, the wind whipping around her face and the sunlight glaring off the lake. She was going to do it! Chelsea turned around again and again and again, her feet hitting the middle of the wake in a strong, perfectly timed whirlybird 720.

She thought all the noise she was hearing must have just been exhilaration and blood rushing in her ears, but when she turned to look at the shore, she saw everyone watching her, clapping and cheering. Her face flushed with happiness and triumph. She had finally done it! It might have taken her all summer, but she had mastered one of the most difficult tricks in the book. It could only get better from there.

"How was that?" Chelsea asked Todd as she climbed back into the boat.

Todd cut the motor so he could turn and devote all his attention to her. He put his arms around her waist and looked at her, smiling. "Well, I don't know. . . . I think your rotation timing was a little off. You may want to try counting it out in your he—"

"Would you just shut up?" Chelsea said, grinning at him as she grabbed him around the waist and pulled him toward her for a long, passionate kiss.

And for once, Chelsea didn't care if the whole resort could see everything she was doing. All she knew was that she was happier than she had ever been before. In the warm summer sunlight, Todd kissed Chelsea back, feeling awake, happy, and alive. The summer season might have been over, but Chelsea knew that her life had just begun.

Tired of crushing on the wrong guys?
Here's an excerpt from Hailey Abbott's

THE PERFECT BOY

Ciara Simmons gripped the back of Dougie Hendrick's neck and pulled him closer as his tongue slid inside her mouth. She closed her eyes and breathed in the mixture of sweat and TAG body spray wafting from his skin as the sun beat down on them through the rear windows of his Hummer, which was parked at the edge of the student parking lot at Westwood Prep.

Ciara's mind traced over the past half hour: Dougie had strolled up as she finished cleaning out her locker, shoving a year's worth of old loose-leaf and worn manila folders into a trash bag and carefully taking down the photos of her and her best friend, Em, rocking out at the Black Eyed Peas show and partying on their class trip to Baja. Star of the lacrosse team and headed for USC, Dougie was a hulking blond senior with a small sun tattoo on the right side of his wide, tan neck. Girls loved him, and Ciara had been making eyes at him from across the room in her Eastern Religions elective for the better part of the semester.

As he approached her locker, Ciara waited for the familiar surge of power and excitement she always got when she was about to "land" a guy. She waited through Dougie telling her that she looked good and that he was sorry he didn't get to know her better while he was still at Westwood. He asked if she wanted to check out the sound system in his new Hummer. As soon as his gaze fluttered from her long, dark legs to her twinkling Hershey-colored eyes, she knew that Dougie wanted to touch her. She waited for this to feel good and right, like it always did. And now, in the hot backseat of the Hummer, with Dougie's arms around her and his tongue halfway down her throat, Ciara was still waiting.

Ever since her first kiss behind the toolshed at the far end of the soccer field in the sixth grade, Ciara loved smooching boys. She loved the way they smelled, loved the curious, longing way their lips moved, loved the way they looked like they would do anything to keep kissing her once she pulled away. She considered herself kind of a player—she liked having guys around, but once the initial rush of that first heady kiss wore off, she tended to get bored. And lately, the boredom was setting in faster and the rush took longer to kick in. Ciara had always prided herself on thinking more like a guy than most of the guys she knew, but lately it seemed like every guy she made out with was getting more out of the experience than she was.

Dougie's fingers, broad and callused from so many hours cradling the lacrosse stick, began to creep under the soft cotton of her lavender Miss Sixty T-shirt. Ciara pulled back, clamping her hand over his through the material.

"Uh-uh," she warned him.

"No?" Dougie flashed the wide, open grin that had probably worked many times on other girls. But she was already tired of his smile and his need. She was ready to be out of there.

"Sorry, I don't play that way," Ciara said, removing his hand and scooting away from him on the seat. She stretched her arms over her head, then checked the small gold Seiko watch she always wore on her left wrist. "In fact, I should get going. I gotta start packing."

"Oh. Well, uh, where are you off to?" Dougie asked. He sounded disappointed. She could hardly blame him—he probably thought he was going to score a goal, and she was already calling game over.

"Santa Barbara," Ciara said. "My dad's got a place near the beach." There was no reason for Dougie to know her dad had been living in their summer house permanently ever since her parents split up right after Christmas. That was the kind of thing you only told best friends, not casual hookups.

"You gonna be away all summer?" Dougie asked, reaching for her again. The heat inside the car had plastered his blond hair against his forehead with sweat, and his eyes looked puffy in the harsh sunlight. To Ciara, he suddenly didn't look nearly as good as he had standing by her locker in the hallway half an hour before.

"Maybe." She shrugged halfheartedly. "Maybe not. We'll see."

"Well, how 'bout giving me your number for when you get back in the fall?"

"Who knows if I'm even coming back," Ciara said saucily. She had already grabbed her backpack and opened the door. She hopped out of the car and strode across the parking lot to her cherry-red Jetta. As she slid into the driver's seat, her shoulders began to slump. The high she usually got from landing a guy had never materialized, and the faint scent of TAG body spray in her hair was so cloying it turned her stomach. She couldn't wait to get home and take a shower—even though it would take her thick, kinky hair hours to dry.

Her cell rang as she clicked her seat belt into place.

"Where were you?" Em's voice came floating through the earpiece. "We waited for you after school, but you never showed. We're still on for movie night, aren't we?"

Ciara groaned to herself. Movie night used to be her

favorite thing in the world: her and Em sharing vats of kettle corn and mooning over Heath Ledger's sexy accent until the wee hours. But ever since Em had gotten together with her boyfriend, Tim, right before Valentine's Day, movie night had become a three-person affair, with guns and car chases infiltrating the mix.

"I had some stuff to take care of," Ciara said quietly.

"Oh?" She could hear the skepticism in Em's voice. "Like what? And does this have anything to do with Dougie Hendrick chatting you up at your locker?"

"I guess." Ciara sighed. She felt too beat to lie, and Em would eventually worm the truth out of her anyway.

"I see." Ciara visualized Em's lips pressing together to form a flat, disapproving line. "And let me guess—the two of you ended up in his Hummer? He wanted to 'show you his new stereo'?"

A strong flash of nostalgia for the old Em swept through her. Before she got together with Tim, Em was just like Ciara—they even used to compete to see who could lock lips with the most hotties. But now that she was lost in the world of domestic bliss, Em had begun to disapprove of Ciara's playerly ways.

"So are you going to see Dougie again?" Em continued. Ciara could tell from the tone of her voice that Em already knew the answer. She frowned as she pulled to a stop at a traffic light on La Brea and Melrose.

"I don't think so," Ciara said. "You know my style."

"Love 'em and leave 'em." Em sighed. "I know. Look, don't you think it's time you maybe chilled out a little on that? It wouldn't kill you to get with someone you really cared about for once."

Ciara frowned. It seemed like Em was more up her butt to stop messing around every day. Ciara had to admit that Tim was a pretty great guy, but that didn't mean Ciara had to go out and find one of her own as well.

Em paused. "You know people have been saying some not-so-nice things about you ever since Lauren walked in on you and Kyle making out at that party in the Valley," she said reluctantly.

"I didn't know they were still together!" Ciara protested. "He told me they broke up."

"Well"—Em sounded hesitant—"that's kind of part of the problem. I mean, when all you do is randomly hook up with people, you don't really know whether you can trust them or not."

Ciara told herself she was just irritated with the traffic on Melrose and not with what Em was telling her. "I know what I'm doing," she assured her friend. "I'm sixteen—aren't I allowed to have a little fun?"

Em sighed again. "All I'm saying is that people are starting to talk," she said.

"People can say whatever they want," Ciara snapped, trying to ignore the doubt creeping into her stomach. "But hey, let me go, all right? I'm going to need both hands once I get on the freeway."

"Okay . . . ," Em said. "About tonight. Tim TiVo'd *Godfather* for him and *Save the Last Dance* for us."

"Maybe I'll come," Ciara said. The thought of watching Em and Tim snuggle on the couch all night made her stomach turn. "I'll see how much packing I get done. I want to get an early start tomorrow morning."

"Well, at least call me before you leave," Em said, sounding disappointed.

"I will," Ciara promised, flipping her phone shut and shoving a Lil Jon album into her CD player, hoping the hard, rhythmic music would shove out the bitter taste in her mouth as she battled her way onto the freeway. She tried to pay attention to the beats, but Em's comment about people starting to talk kept fighting for space in her head. She'd always been good about not kissing and telling, but what was the point if the guys decided to talk? Ciara prided herself on the reputation she'd built at Westwood—as a strong, independent leader who never took crap from anyone. She took all honors classes and was on the swim team, student council, debate club, and diversity committee. She didn't go in for cliques and was nice to everyone, even the nerdy boys who played Warhammer in the back of the cafeteria. If she wanted to blow off a little steam by locking lips with a guy or two, what right did that give people to say not-so-nice things? But now that hooking up left her without the old high-flying feeling she used to get out of it, was there even still a point?

Just the thought of it made the slimy tentacles of regret creep farther into her stomach. Once they reached a certain point, she knew they would turn from doubt to guilt. She hated the feeling that she'd done something wrong after hooking up with a guy, but a few hours after the fact, it always came to sit like a lump of cold, flavorless oatmeal in her gut. It wasn't so much worry over what people might be saying (although knowing there was gossip around wasn't exactly the best feeling in the world either) or whether she'd hurt someone's feelings. More than that, it was the lingering doubt that she might somehow be hurting *herself*, doing some permanent damage that would only become apparent in the future, when all her friends were getting married and she'd find out she was some kind of freak incapable of having a normal relationship.

"You're being stupid," she reprimanded herself as she pulled off the freeway at Santa Monica. "It's the twenty-first century, you're an independent operator, and you like to kiss a boy or two every now and then without a major commitment. It's not like marrying the first guy who comes along is a great idea either. Look at Britney!"

She'd almost rationalized away the lump in her stomach as she pulled into her driveway. Ever since her dad had moved out, the house felt too big for just her and her mom. It was always a faint letdown when she came home and heard her footsteps echo hollowly on the polished marble tiles of the front foyer. When her dad had lived there, his large, booming presence filled the house even when he wasn't home. He seemed to leave pieces of himself everywhere—his shoes in the entryway, his keys on the kitchen table, magazines and papers strewn throughout the living room. Her mom was much neater. Ciara didn't know how she managed to keep the house so clean while working at the ad agency every night until nine or ten, but nothing was ever out of place anymore. Nothing except for Ciara's dad's absence.

There was a note from her mom telling her she'd be at work late (again) and to call for takeout if she got hungry. Ciara sighed. When she was a kid, her mom always found ways to get in family time around her job, like sneaking Ciara on business trips and ordering room service from the fancy hotels they stayed at. But ever since the divorce, her mom had thrown herself into her job to the exclusion of practically everything else. She had always been kind of a workaholic, but in the past few months, she'd spent entire nights at the office, sometimes driving home only to shower and change her clothes. Ciara supposed she got her über-driven nature from her mom, who had fought tooth and nail to climb the competitive ladder of the advertising world ever since moving to LA from Peru as a teenager and marrying

Ciara's dad at the age of twenty-two.

Ciara crumpled up the note and lobbed it into the trash before trudging up the stairs to her room. She dragged her suitcase down from the top of her closet and turned on the radio to 100.3 The Beat, her favorite hip-hop station. Ciara loved music that made her get up and move: Her iPod was packed to bursting with bouncy hip-hop, from Q-Tip and OutKast to Diddy and 50 Cent, and her dream was to become an entertainment lawyer so she could represent all her favorite stars. The new Beyoncé played as she threw bikinis, sarongs, and flip-flops into her suitcase, trying to concentrate on how great it would be to hit the beaches in Santa Barbara. But the smell of Dougie's cologne on her hair and the echo of Em's words in her head kept distracting her, and the post-hookup nastiness thudded in her stomach.

She realized that what she was looking forward to most about spending the summer in Santa Barbara wasn't hitting some of the cleanest beaches on the West Coast, but getting away from the mess her life had become in LA. In Santa Barbara, she could get some distance and perspective, maybe get a fresh start. There would be no Dougies trying to lure her into backseats, no Em and Tim lording their couplehood over her, no guys with big mouths telling all their friends about the last time they'd hooked up. In Santa Barbara, she could be whoever she wanted to be. If only she knew who that was. . . .

"And now for a trip back to the nineties," said the announcer's voice on the radio as the Beyoncé song faded. "Who's ready for Big Pun?"

The opening chords to "Still Not a Player" came booming through her speakers, and Ciara froze with a lavender bikini in her hand. She hadn't heard that song since she was in middle school. "I don't wanna be a player no more," went the chorus.

"Hey!" Ciara yelled, spinning to address her speakers. "Just what are you trying to imply?"

"Player no more," crooned the background singers.

Ciara knew it was silly, but she couldn't help wondering if this was some sort of sign that her behavior was getting to be too much. If Big Pun was ready to stop being a player, did that mean she should be, too?

"It's hard to be a player when you're dead like Big Pun," she reminded herself. Just then, the breeze from her open window blew a strand of her hair into her face—and the gross scent of Dougie's TAG with it. The regret returned with full force, squeezing her chest. Maybe, she thought, just maybe she should give this whole random hookup thing a rest.

*   *   *

Ciara loved the trip up US Highway 101 from Los Angeles to Santa Barbara. The road snaked along the coast, coming into kissing contact with the ocean from time to time: the perfect drive to make with your sunroof open and the windows down, singing along to your favorite hip-hop station on a beautiful afternoon in early summer.

It was weird to be making the journey alone, though. When her parents first bought the summer house, they drove there almost every weekend in the spring and fall, her dad blasting old Motown hits and whistling off-key. They always let Ciara sit up front so her mom could have the entire backseat to spread out her files and type away on her laptop.

Ciara spent two great summers at the house before starting high school, hanging out on the beach every day with Heidi, Marlene, Kevin, and AJ, the friends she'd met at the private beach club her parents joined. As the ocean swooped back into view, she lazily wondered if they were still around.

By the time she got to high school, though, Ciara had to say good-bye to her Santa Barbara summers. As a future entertainment lawyer determined to get into an Ivy League college, Ciara packed her weekends with volunteer work and extracurricular activities, leaving no time to head up to the beach house and chill. Forget summers: Going into ninth grade, she was a CIT at a day camp for underprivileged children, and the summer after that, she got an internship at Deuter Schlosselman,

LLP, one of the top entertainment law firms in LA. She'd meant to at least head up to the house for a weekend but had gotten so busy the time just never materialized.

But this summer would be different, Ciara promised herself. No grueling internships: Instead, she would get a part-time job and save money for college while still having time for fun. She would put the difficult, disastrous past few months at Westwood Prep behind her and focus on making friends, checking out great music, and getting a killer tan. Just thinking about it lifted the cloud of stress and misery that had accumulated around her like the dense LA smog. She reminded herself that nobody in Santa Barbara had seen her since she was thirteen. They didn't know about her escapades in upstairs bedrooms at parties or in the backseats of Hummers in the student parking lot. She'd be far away from all of that—and from that big empty house in LA she'd come to feel so lost in lately.

Ciara laughed to herself as she thought of all the lame guys she was leaving behind at Westwood. Maybe they grew them differently in Santa Barbara—the fresh air and proximity to the ocean had to be worth something, didn't it? Wind whipped her hair through the open window, and she pictured legions of ripped dudes on surfboards just waiting to show her how deep, broad, and cool the SB dating pool could be.

Perfect town, perfect job, perfect summer, perfect guy . . . Ciara's mind reeled with the possibilities. She could leave behind the mess her life had become in LA and unveil a new Ciara who did everything right. And then . . . well, why go back home at all? Why not just stay in Santa Barbara with her dad and her new, perfect life? She was being handed a chance to change on a silver platter—and she was determined to make it work.

As the miles sped by under the wheels of her Jetta, 100.3 started to get staticky and fade out. Ciara hit browse on the radio, letting it flip past country and Latin stations. A familiar beat caught her ear, and she almost swerved out of her lane when she realized what it was.

Why was "Still Not a Player" on the radio *again*?!

Ciara tried to rationalize that maybe it was Big Pun's birthday or the anniversary of his death or something. Why else would a song from nearly ten years ago be in such heavy rotation? But a nagging voice in her head told her that it was more than a coincidence: It seemed like a sign. She had to admit that she'd been up tossing and turning for much of the night before, and not just in anticipation of the trip to Santa Barbara. Em's statement that people were talking hadn't stopped echoing in her head.

It wasn't so much that she liked cultivating an endless string of random hookups. In a way, she was jealous of Em and Tim's relationship. It might be nice to have someone be there no matter what—someone who could be a best friend as well as a warm body and a pair of lips. It was just that she had never met a guy who seemed worth taking things further than that magical first kiss. She had always joked with Em that the perfect guy would have to be as driven as herself and hotter than Bow Wow . . . and good luck finding *that* at Westwood Prep!

Still, something about her "love-'em-and-leave-'em" approach wasn't working the way that it used to. With every guy she kissed, the high was shorter and the nasty post-hookup feeling more intense. Now that rumors were starting to follow her around, maybe it was time to stop being a player after all.

The thought made her hands go clammy on the steering wheel. It would be a challenge to change her ways—she was a natural flirt and loved attention. On the other hand, the emptiness she felt afterward was getting harder and harder to bear.

Rounding the bend heading toward Mussel Shoals, Ciara made a vow to herself to curb her hookup habit until she found someone worth taking things farther than the first kiss. This summer, she would either get with the perfect guy or no one at all.

Read these juicy summer page-turners!

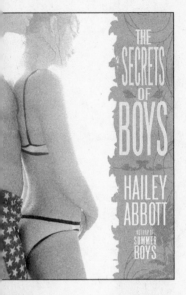

The Secrets of Boys

A California girl like Cassidy Jones should be out on the beach, not stuck in summer school! But her life heats up when she meets the worldly and romantic Zach—she can't stop thinking about him, even though she already has a boyfriend. Cassidy wishes her pal Joe was around to help her figure out the secrets of boys, but he's hundreds of miles away. Will she be able to ignore her feelings for Zach—or will temptation be too strong to resist?

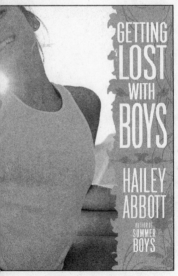

Getting Lost with Boys

Cordelia Packer hates the unexpected, but she's in for a surprise when Jacob Stein offers to be her travel companion, all the way from San Diego to her sister's place in Northern California. Before she knows it, her neatly laid out summer plan has turned into a wild road trip, where anything can—and does—happen. Who knew getting lost with a boy could be so much fun?